4

BY

PELEVIN

*Also by Victor Pelevin
from New Directions*

THE BLUE LANTERN

OMON RA

THE YELLOW ARROW

A WEREWOLF PROBLEM IN CENTRAL
RUSSIA

VICTOR PELEVIN

4 BY PELEVIN

STORIES

Translated from the Russian
by Andrew Bromfield

A NEW DIRECTIONS
Bibelot

Manufactured in the United States of America
New Directions Books are printed on acid-free paper.
First published as a New Directions Bibelot in 2001
Published simultaneously in Canada by Penguin Books Canada Limited

Library of Congress-in-Publication Data

Pelevin, Viktor.
    [Short stories. English. Selections]
    Four by Pelevin: stories / Victor Pelevin; translated by Andrew Bromfield.
        p.cm.
            Contents: Hermit and Six Toes – The Life and Adventures of Shed Number XII –
    Vera Pavlovna's Ninth Dream – Tai Shou Chuan USSR (A Chinese Folktale).
        ISBN 0-8112-1491-5 (alk. paper)
1. Pelevin, Viktor—Translations into English. I. Bromfield, Andrew. II. Title.

PG3485.E38 A23 2001
891.73'44—dc21   2001031686

New Directions Books are published for James Laughlin
by New Directions Publishing Corporation
80 Eighth Avenue, New York 10011

Contents

HERMIT AND SIX-TOES 1

THE LIFE AND ADVENTURES OF SHED NUMBER XII 45

VERA PAVLOVNA'S NINTH DREAM 59

TAI SHOU CHUAN USSR (A CHINESE FOLK TALE) 85

4

BY

PELEVIN

HERMIT
AND
SIX-TOES

"Get lost!"

"What?"

"I said, get lost. Out of my way, I'm trying to watch."

"What're you watching?"

"God, what an idiot. . . . All right, the sun."

Six-Toes lifted his gaze from the black surface of the soil, scattered with food, sawdust, and powdered peat, screwed up his eyes, and stared into the sky.

"Yeah . . . we just keep living our lives, but what's it all for? The mystery of the ages. Who has ever truly comprehended the subtle filiform essence of the lights of heaven?"

The stranger turned his head and contemplated him with an expression of curious disgust.

"Six-Toes," said Six-Toes immediately, introducing himself.

"I'm Hermit," replied the stranger. "Is that the way they talk here in your community? *Subtle filiform essence?*"

"Not my community anymore," answered Six-Toes, and then suddenly gave a whistle: "Hey, will you look at that!"

"What?" Hermit asked suspiciously.

"Look, up there! Another one's just appeared!"

"What of it?"

"That never happens in the center of the world. Three suns all at once."

Hermit sniggered condescendingly. "I've seen eleven of them at once. One at zenith and five in each epicycle. Of course, that wasn't here."

"Where was it?" asked Six-Toes.

Hermit didn't answer. He turned, walked away, and picking up a food scrap from the ground with his foot, began to eat. There was a warm, gentle wind, and two suns were reflected in the grey-green planes of the distant horizon. In this atmosphere of calm sadness Hermit became so engrossed in his thoughts that when he suddenly noticed Six-Toes standing in front of him he shuddered in surprise. "You again! Well, what do you want?"

"Nothing. I just feel like talking."

"You don't seem any too bright to me. You should get back to the community. You've wandered too far away. Go on, go back over there. . . ." He waved in the direction of a thin dirty-yellow line wriggling and trembling in the distance. It was hard to believe that was how the huge unruly crowd appeared from here.

"I would go back," said Six-Toes, "but they threw me out."

"Really? What for? Politics?"

Six-Toes nodded, scratching one leg with the other. Hermit glanced down at his feet and nodded.

"Are they real?"

"What else could they be? What they said to me was, Here we are just coming up to the Decisive Stage, and there you are with six toes on your feet. . . . Real good timing, they said. . . ."

"What 'Decisive Stage' is that?"

"I don't know. All of them milling about with long faces, especially the Twenty Closest, and I don't understand a thing. All of them running around, yelling and shouting."

"Ah," said Hermit, "I understand. No doubt it gets clearer and clearer by the hour? Gradually assuming visible shape and form?"

"That's right," said Six-Toes, astonished. "How did you know?"

"I've already seen five of these Decisive Stages. Only they all had different names."

"But how can that be?" said Six-Toes. "I know this is the first time it's happened."

"Of course it is. It would be rather interesting to see what happens the second time around. . . . But then we're talking about somewhat different things." Laughing quietly, Hermit took a few steps towards the distant community, turned his back to it, and began scraping up the ground with his feet. Very soon a cloud of sawdust, peat, and scraps of food had formed in the air behind his back. He kept glancing round, waving his arms in the air, and muttering to himself. Six-Toes felt a bit frightened.

"What were you doing?" he asked, when Hermit came back over to him, breathing heavily.

"It's a gesture," Hermit answered. "An art form. You read a poem and perform the actions to go with it."

"Which poem did you read?"

"This one," said Hermit:

"Sometimes I feel sad
Observing those I have left.
Sometimes I laugh,
And then between us
There rises up the yellow mist."

"That's not a poem," said Six-Toes. "I know all of the poems, thank God. Not by heart, of course, but I've heard all twenty-five of them. That definitely isn't one of them."

Hermit looked at him in surprise, and then seemed to understand.

"Can you remember at least one?" he asked. "Recite one for me."

"Just a moment. The twins . . . The twins . . . right,

well, to cut it short, it's about how we say one thing and we mean another. And then we say one thing and mean another again, only like the other way round. It's all very beautiful. At the end we look up at the wall and see a face that puts an end to all doubt and hesitation—"

"Enough!" Hermit interrupted.

There was silence.

Six-Toes was the first to break it: "So, did they throw you out too?"

"No, I threw all of them out."

"How could that happen?"

"All sorts of thing can happen," said Hermit. Glancing up at one of the heavenly bodies, he went on in a tone that suggested a shift from idle chatter to serious conversation: "It'll get dark soon."

"Oh, sure. Right," replied Six-Toes. "Nobody knows when it's going to get dark."

"I know. And if you want to sleep in peace, you just do what I do."

Hermit set about scraping into heaps the sawdust, peat, and various bits of garbage under his feet. Gradually a wall took shape, about the same height as himself, and enclosing a small distinct space. His construction completed, Hermit stepped back, glanced at it lovingly, and said: "There. I call it The Sanctuary of the Soul."

"Why?" asked Six-Toes."

"I like the sound of it. Are you going to build one?"

Six-Toes began scratching and scraping, but he couldn't get the hang of it. His wall kept collapsing. To tell the truth, he wasn't trying very hard, because he didn't really believe what Hermit had told him about it getting dark, so when the lights of heaven wavered and began gradually to dim, and the distant community gave out a communal gasp of horror like the wind rustling through straw, he was simultaneously overcome by two powerful feelings: the usual terror at the sudden advance of darkness and an unfamiliar feeling of admiration for someone who knew more than he did about the world.

"So be it," said Hermit. "You jump inside and I'll build another one."

"I don't know how to jump," Six-Toes answered in a quiet voice.

"So long, then," said Hermit. Suddenly he pushed off from the earth with all his strength, soared up into the air, and disappeared behind his wall. Then the entire structure collapsed in on him, covering him with an even layer of sawdust and peat. The small hillock that was formed in this way carried on shuddering for a little while, and then a little opening appeared in its side. Six-Toes just caught a glimpse of Hermit's eyes glittering in it before total darkness descended.

For as long as he could remember, Six-Toes had of course known all he needed to know about night. "It's a natural process," some said. "We should just get on with our work," said others, the majority. There were many shades of opinion, but the same thing happened to everyone regardless. When the light disappeared without any apparent cause, after struggling briefly and helplessly against the paralyzing terror, they all fell into a state of torpor, and when they came to—when the lights began shining again—they could remember almost nothing. When Six-Toes was still living in the community, the same thing had happened to him, but now, probably because his terror at the onset of night was overlaid and doubled by his terror at being alone, the standard salvation of a coma was denied him. In the distance the community had fallen silent, but he just went on sitting there, conscious, hunched over, beside the mound, crying quietly. He couldn't see a thing, and when Hermit's voice suddenly pierced the darkness, he was so frightened that he shat right there on the spot.

"Hey, stop that banging, will you?" Hermit complained. "I can't sleep."

"I'm not banging," Six-Toes answered in a quiet voice. "It's my heart. Talk to me for a bit, will you?"

"What about?" asked Hermit.

"Anything you like, just make it as long as you can."

"How about the nature of fear, then?"

"Oh, no, not that," squeaked Six-Toes.

"Quiet!" hissed Hermit. "Or we'll have all the rats here in a moment."

"Rats? What are they?" Six-Toes asked in cold fright.

"Creatures of the night. And of the day too, for that matter."

"Life has been cruel to me," whispered Six-Toes. "If only I had the right number of toes, I'd be sleeping with all the others. God, I'm so afraid. . . . Rats. . . ,"

"Listen," said Hermit, "you keep on saying God this, God that—do they believe in God over there, then?"

"God only knows. There is something, that's for sure, but just what, nobody knows. For instance, why does it get dark? If you like you can explain it by natural causes, of course. And if you go thinking about God, you'll never get anything done in this life . . ."

"So just what can you get done in this life?"

"What a question! Why do you ask stupid questions, as if you don't know the answers already? Everyone tries as hard as he can to get to the trough. It's the law of life."

"Okay. Then what's it all for?"

"All what?"

"You know, the universe, the sky, the earth, the suns, all of it."

"What d'you mean, what for? That's just the way the world is."

"What way is it?" Hermit asked in a curious voice.

"Just the way it is. We move in space and time. According to the laws of life."

"Where to?"

"How should I know? It's the mystery of the ages. You're enough to drive anyone crazy."

"You're the one who'd drive anyone crazy. No matter what we talk about, it's all the law of life or the mystery of the ages."

"If you don't like it," said Six-Toes, offended, "then don't talk."

"I wouldn't be talking if you weren't afraid of the dark."

Six-Toes had completely forgotten about that. He focused on what he was feeling, and suddenly realized there was no fear there at all. This frightened him so much that he leapt to his feet and set off running blindly into the darkness, until his head slammed at full speed into the invisible Wall of the World.

In the distance Six-Toes could hear Hermit's cackling laughter. Placing one foot carefully in front of the other, he began making his way towards it, the only sound in the silent, impenetrable darkness that surrounded him. When he reached the mound in which Hermit was ensconced, he lay down beside it without a word and tried to ignore the cold and go to sleep. He didn't even notice when he finally did.

II

"Today we're going to climb over the Wall of the World, okay?" said Hermit.

Six-Toes was just making the approach to his sanctuary of the soul. The actual structure now turned out just like Hermit's, but he could only manage the jump by a long run up to it, and he was practising. The meaning of Hermit's words penetrated just at the moment of takeoff, with the result that he hurtled straight into the shaky construction, and the peat and sawdust, instead of settling over his body in a smooth, soft layer, ended up as an untidy heap on top of his head, while his feet stuck helplessly up into the air. Hermit helped him to scramble out and then said it again:

"Today we're going over the Wall of the World."

In the last few days Six-Toes had heard so many incredible things from Hermit that his mind was in a constant state of groaning turmoil, and his old life in the community seemed no more than an amusing fantasy—or perhaps a vulgar nightmare, he hadn't quite decided yet. But this was just too much.

Hermit carried on: "The Decisive Stage comes round after every seventy eclipses. Yesterday was the sixty-ninth. The world is ruled by numbers." He pointed to a long chain made of linked straws protruding from the earth right beside the Wall of the World.

"But how can we climb over the Wall of the World if it's the Wall of the World? The very name . . . I mean, there isn't anything on the other side. . . ."

Six-Toes was so flabbergasted by the very idea that he didn't hear a word of Hermit's dark mystical explanations, which would only have upset him even more anyway.

"So what if there isn't anything?" answered Hermit. "We should be glad of it."

"But what will we do there?"

"Live."

"What's so bad about here?"

"The fact that soon there won't be any more 'here' here, you idiot."

"Then what will there be?"

"You stay here and you'll find out soon enough. There won't be anything."

Six-Toes realized he had completely lost his bearings.

"Why are you always frightening me like this?"

"Stop whining, will you?" muttered Hermit, gazing up anxiously at some point in the sky. "Things are okay on the other side of the Wall of the World. I'd say they're a lot better than here."

He walked over to the remains of the sanctuary Six-Toes had built and began scattering them in all directions with his feet.

"What're you doing that for?" Six-Toes asked.

"Before departing from any world, you have to summarize the experience of existence there and then destroy all traces of your presence."

"Who made that up?"

"What does it matter? Okay, I did. There isn't anyone else around here to do things like that. So. . . ."

Hermit contemplated the result of his labors. The site of the collapsed structure was now perfectly smooth and quite indistinguishable from the surrounding surface of the desert.

"That's done," he said. "I've destroyed the traces. Now we have to summarize our experience. It's your turn. Climb up on that tussock and tell me about it."

Six-Toes felt like he was being tricked into doing the most difficult job, the one that was hardest to grasp, but after what happened with the eclipse he'd decided he'd better do what Hermit said. He glanced around with a shrug to make sure no one from the community had wandered over in their direction, and then clambered on to the tussock.

"What do I talk about?"

"Everything you know about the world."

"We'll be stuck here quite a while, then," said Six-Toes with a whistle.

"I doubt it," Hermit replied drily.

"All right, then. Our world. . . . This ritual of yours is plain stupid. . . ."

"Get on with it."

"Our world is a regular octagon moving at a regular speed along a linear course through space. Here we prepare ourselves for the Decisive Stage, the crowning event of our lives. At least, that's the official formula. Around the perimeter of the world runs the Wall of the World, which is the objective result of the operation of the laws of life. In the center of the world stands the combined feed-trough and drinking-trough, on which our civilization has been centered since time immemorial. The position of a member of the community relative to the troughs is determined by his social standing and his merits—"

"I've not heard that part before," Hermit interrupted. "What are these merits, and what's social standing?"

"Well. . . . How can I explain it? It's when someone actually reaches the trough."

"And who does reach it?"

"I told you, the ones who have the greatest merits. Or the highest social standing. Take me, for instance, I used to have kind of average merits, but now I don't have any. You mean to say you don't know the popular model of the universe?"

"No, I don't," said Hermit.

"Oh, come on. . . . So how come you were preparing for the Decisive Stage?"

"I'll tell you later. Carry on."

"That's almost all there is. What else is there? Beyond the province of the community lies the great desert, and everything ends in the Wall of the World. Turncoats like us take refuge by the wall."

"Turncoats. Okay. So which way round should the coat be? Where's the tailor?"

"There you go again. . . . Not even the Twenty Closest can tell you that. It's the mystery of the ages."

"Okay, then. So what's the mystery of the ages?"

"The law of life," Six-Toes answered, trying to keep his voice down. Something in Hermit's tone of voice made him feel uneasy.

"All right. And what's the law of life?"

"It's the mystery of the ages."

"The *mystery* of the ages," Hermit repeated in a strange, thin voice, and he began slowly circling towards Six-Toes.

"You stop that!" Six-Toes shouted from fear. "You and your ritual!"

But Hermit had already gotten a grip on himself.

"Okay," he said. "Get down."

Six-Toes climbed down from the tussock, and Hermit clambered up to take his place, wearing an expression of serious concentration. For a while he said nothing, as though listening carefully to something, then he raised his head and began.

"I came here from another world," he said, "in the days when you were still very small. I came to that other world from a third world, and so on. I have been in five worlds in all. They are all just like this one, with almost nothing to distinguish them from each other. The universe in which we find ourselves consists of an immense enclosed space. In the language of the gods it is known as 'the Lunacharsky Broiler Combine,' but what that means even they do not know."

"You know the language of the gods?" Six-Toes asked in amazement.

"A little. Don't interrupt. There are seventy worlds altogether in the universe. We are in one of them at the moment. These worlds are fastened to an endless black belt which moves slowly in a circle. Above it, on the surface of the sky, there are hundreds of identical suns. They do not move over us, it is we who move below them. Try to picture it."

Six-Toes closed his eyes, a strained expression dawning on his face.

"No, I can't," he said eventually.

"Okay," said Hermit. "Listen. All of the seventy worlds in the universe are together known as the Chain of Worlds. At least, they can be called that. In each of the worlds there is life, but it does not exist continuously, it appears and disappears in cycles. The Decisive Stage occurs in the center of the universe, through which all of the worlds pass in turn. In the language of the gods it is known as Shop Number One. At the moment our world is located at its very threshold. When the Decisive Stage is concluded and the world emerges renewed from the far side of Shop Number One, everything starts all over again. Life appears, runs through its cycle and at the appointed time it is plunged back into Shop Number One."

"How do you know all this?" Six-Toes asked in a half-whisper.

"I've traveled around a lot," said Hermit, "and picked up the secret knowledge crumb by crumb. In one world they knew one thing, in another something else."

"Maybe you know where we come from?"

"Yes, I do. But what do they say about that in your world?"

"They say it's an objective given—the law of life."

"I see. You're asking me about one of the most profound mysteries of the universe and I'm not even sure I can trust you with it. But since there isn't anyone else around, I suppose I'll tell you anyway. We appear in this world out of white spheres. They're not actually spheres, they're slightly elongated, and one end is narrower than the other, but that's not important right now."

"Spheres. White spheres," repeated Six-Toes, and then he suddenly keeled over and his body hit the ground. The burden of what he had learnt descended on him like a physical weight, and for a second he thought he was going to die. Hermit jumped down and began to shake him with all his might. Six-Toes gradually regained some clarity of mind.

"What's wrong with you?" Hermit asked, alarmed.

"Oh, I remembered. That's how it was. We used to be white spheres lying on long shelves in a place that was very warm and damp. And then from inside we began breaking open the spheres and . . . our world came up from somewhere below us, and then we were already in it. . . . But why doesn't anyone remember all this?"

"There are worlds in which they remember," said Hermit. "It's only the fifth and sixth prenatal matrix. Not really all that deep, and only one part of the truth. But even so they isolate the ones who remember it, so they won't interfere with the preparations for the Decisive Stage, or whatever it happens to be called. It has a different name in every world. In my world, for instance, it was known as the Completion of Construction, although no one there ever built anything at all."

Clearly overcome by sadness at the memory of his own world, Hermit fell silent.

"Listen," Six-Toes said after a little while, "where do the white spheres come from?"

Hermit looked at him approvingly.

"Before I was ready to ask that question," he said, "I needed much more time. But this is where things get much more complicated. One ancient legend says that these eggs appear from within us, but that could just be a metaphor. . . ."

"From within us? I don't understand. Where did you hear that?"

"I made it up myself. Where could you hear anything around here?" Hermit said in a voice that suddenly sounded weary.

"But you said it was an ancient legend."

"That's right. I made it up as an ancient legend."

"What d'you mean? What for?"

"You see, an ancient sage, you could call him a prophet"— this time Six-Toes guessed who was meant—"once said that what matters is not what is said, but who says it. Part of the meaning I was trying to express is that my words fulfil the function of an ancient legend. But how can you be expected. . . ." Hermit glanced up at the sky and interrupted his own train of thought: "Enough of that. It's time to go."

"Go where?"

"To the community."

Six-Toes gawped at him. "We were going to climb over the Wall of the World. What do we need the community for?"

"Don't you have any idea what the community really is?" Hermit asked. "It is precisely a device for climbing over the Wall of the World."

III

Although there was not a single object you could hide behind in the desert, Six-Toes crept along furtively, and the closer they came to the community, the more obviously criminal his stride became. Gradually the huge crowd, which from a distance had seemed like a single wriggling creature, disintegrated into individual bodies; they could even make out scowls of astonishment on the faces which had noticed them approaching.

"The main thing," Hermit whispered, repeating his final instruction, "is to be insolent, but not too insolent. We have to make them mad, but not so mad that they tear us to pieces. Just keep an eye on what I do."

"Hey, Six-Toes is back!" someone ahead of them shouted cheerfully. "You old bastard! Hey, Six-Toes, who's that with you?"

For some strange reason at the sound of this muddle-headed abuse Six-Toes was overwhelmed by nostalgic childhood memories. Hermit, walking right behind him, seemed to sense this, and he poked Six-Toes in the back. The individuals on the very edge of the community were quite widely separated. This was where the cripples and the contemplatives lived, the ones who did not like to be crowded, and it was easy to make your way past them. But the further they went, the denser the crowd became, and very soon Hermit and Six-Toes found themselves in an unbearable crush. It was still possible to move forward, but only at the cost of squabbling with your neighbors, and by the time that the trembling roof of the troughs had appeared above the heads of the crowd in front of them, it was impossible to take another step forward.

"It never ceases to amaze me," Hermit said quietly to Six-Toes, "just how wisely everything is arranged here. Those who stand closest to the troughs are happy, mostly because they are constantly thinking about the others who want to take their place. And those who wait all their lives for a narrow crack to appear between the bodies up in front are happy because they have something to hope for. That is harmony and unity."

"Anything wrong with that?" asked a voice from one side.

"Yes, I don't like it," answered Hermit.

"And just what is it that you don't like?"

"All of it." Hermit made a sweeping gesture which took in the crowd, the majestic dome of the troughs, the glittering yellow light in the sky and, away in the distance, the barely visible Wall of the World.

"I see. So where is it any better?"

"Nowhere, that's what's so tragic!" Hermit screamed in a martyred voice. "That's the whole problem! If there was anywhere better, why would I waste my time here, discussing life with you?"

"And does your comrade share these views?" asked the voice. "Why is he staring at the ground?"

Six-Toes looked up—he had been gazing down at his feet, because that way he could keep his involvement in what was happening to the minimum—and saw the owner of the voice. He had a fat, flabby face, and when he spoke the anatomical details of his larynx were clearly visible. Six-Toes immediately realized that he was facing one of the Twenty Closest, the living conscience of the era.

"The reason you're so miserable, my young friends," he said, in an unexpectedly friendly tone, "is that you're not preparing for the Decisive Stage along with everybody else. If you were, you wouldn't have time for such thoughts. Even I sometimes have such thoughts. . . . You know, our only salvation lies in work." Then, in exactly the same tone he concluded: "Take them."

There was a movement in the crowd, and Hermit and Six-Toes immediately found themselves hemmed in tightly on all sides.

"We don't give a damn about you," Hermit said in an equally friendly voice. "Where are you going to take us? You have nowhere to take us. All you can do is banish us again. In the words of the old proverb, 'You can't just toss it over the Wall of the World'."

At this point an expression of confused anxiety appeared on Hermit's face, the flabby-faced individual raised his eyebrows, and their eyes met.

"Now there's an interesting idea. We haven't tried that before. The proverb does exist, of course, but the will of the people is stronger."

He was clearly exhilarated by the idea. He turned away and started giving orders.

"Attention! Everybody into line! We're going to do something we hadn't planned on."

It didn't take very long from the moment Flabby-Face issued his order to line up the procession for approaching the Wall of the World and lead Hermit and Six-Toes along at its center.

The procession was impressive. The flabby-faced individual walked at its head, followed by two specially appointed Old Mothers (nobody, including Flabby-Face, knew what their title meant—it was just a tradition), who shouted abuse at Hermit and Six-Toes through their tears, mourning and cursing them at the same time. Next came the two criminals themselves, and bringing up the rear was the common crowd.

"And so," said Flabby-Face, once the procession had stopped, "the fearful moment of retribution is upon us. I am sure, my friends, that we shall all be fighting back our tears when these two turncoats vanish into nonexistence, won't we? And may this alarming event serve as a terrible warning to all of us, to the whole community. . . . Sob louder, Mothers!"

The Old Mothers fell down to the ground and burst into such mournful wailing that many of those present turned away and began swallowing hard. From time to time, however, the Mothers would leap up with eyes blazing from their squirming in the tear-spattered dust and hurl the most terrible and irrefutable accusations at Hermit and Six-Toes, before they collapsed again.

"So, have you repented?" Flabby-Face asked after a little while, "Have the Mothers' tears not roused your sense of shame?"

"I should think so," Hermit answered, shifting his keen gaze from the ceremony to the heavenly bodies and then back again. "How do you intend to throw us over?"

The flabby-faced individual pondered the question. The Old

Mothers fell silent too, then one of them got up out of the dust, shook herself off, and said: "Maybe a ramp?"

"A ramp," said Hermit. "That would take five eclipses. And we are impatient to conceal our unmasked shame in the void."

The flabby-faced individual screwed up his eyes, glanced at Hermit, and nodded approvingly.

"They understand," he said to one of his own people, "they're just pretending. Ask them if they have anything to suggest themselves."

A few minutes later a living pyramid reached up almost to the very top of the Wall of the World. The ones on the top screwed up their eyes and hid their faces in order not to glance out there, at the end of everything.

"Up!" someone shouted at Hermit and Six-Toes, and they started climbing up the precarious rows of shoulders and backs, supporting each other as they made their way towards the top of the wall lost in the distance above their heads.

From the top they could see the entire silent community, carefully watching what was happening from a distance, and could make out certain details of the sky that had not been visible before. They noticed the thick hose that descended out of infinity into the troughs—it didn't look as magnificent from up here as it did from the ground. Leaping up lightly onto the top of the Wall of the World as though onto a mere tussock, Hermit helped Six-Toes to take a seat beside him and shouted down: "Everything's in order!"

At the sound of his shout someone in the pyramid lost his balance; it swayed a few times and then collapsed. Everyone in it went tumbling down to the foot of the wall.

Clutching the cold sheet metal, Six-Toes gazed down at the tiny faces looking up to him, and at the cheerless grey-brown expanses of his homeland. He gazed at the corner of his homeland where there was a large green spot on the Wall of the World, where he had spent his childhood. "I'll never see any of this again," he thought, and even though he wished he wouldn't, he felt a lump rise in his throat. He pressed against his side a small piece of earth with a straw stuck in it, and pondered how rapidly and inexorably everything in his life was changing.

"Goodbye, our sons!" the Old Mothers shouted up from below, first bowing down to the earth and then sobbing as they threw heavy pieces of peat up at them.

Hermit raised himself up on tiptoe and shouted loudly:

"I always knew
That I would quit
This heartless world—"

At this point, he was struck by a large piece of peat, and he tumbled backwards off the wall. Six-Toes cast a final glance below over everything that he was leaving behind, and noticed someone waving to him from the distant crowd. He waved back. Then, closing his eyes tightly, he took a step backwards.

For a few seconds he tumbled untidily through empty space, then with a sudden painful impact he landed on something hard and opened his eyes. He was lying on a black shiny surface of some unfamiliar material. Rising up above him was the Wall of the World, looking just the same as it had on the other side, and beside him, his arm extended towards the wall, stood Hermit. He was completing his recitation of the poem:

"—But that it would be thus
I had no inkling. . . ."

IV

Now that they were walking along the gigantic black belt, Six-Toes could see that Hermit had told him the truth. The belt and the world they had just left really were moving slowly in relation to other cosmic objects fixed in space (the nature of which Six-

Toes could not understand), and the suns were motionless—once you stepped off the black belt it was all quite clear.

The world they had left was now slowly being drawn towards a pair of green steel gates which the belt ran under. Hermit said that was the entrance to Shop Number One. Strangely enough, Six-Toes was not in the least overawed by the magnificence of the objects filling the universe; in fact he felt a certain mild irritation. "Is that all there is?" he thought, vaguely disgusted. In the distance he could see two worlds like the one that they had just left. They were also moving along on the black belt and from where he stood they looked rather squalid. At first Six-Toes thought he and Hermit were on their way to another world, but when they were halfway there, Hermit told him to jump from the motionless border of the moving belt along which they were walking down into a dark, bottomless crevice.

"It's soft," he said to Six-Toes, but Six-Toes took a step backwards, shaking his head. Without another word, Hermit jumped himself, and there was nothing left for Six-Toes but to leap after him.

This time he almost broke something on the hard, cold surface of large brown slabs of stone. The slabs extended off as far as the horizon, and for the first time in his life Six-Toes understood the meaning of the word "infinity."

"What is it?" Six-Toes asked.

"Tiles," Hermit answered him with a meaningless word, and then changed the subject. "The night will begin soon, and we have to get all the way across there. We'll have to go part of the way in darkness."

Hermit seemed seriously concerned about something. Gazing off into the distance Six-Toes was able to make out some yellow cube-shaped rocks—Hermit told him they were called "boxes." There were plenty of them, and the spaces between them he could see were strewn with light-colored wood shavings. From the distance it all looked like a scene from some dimly remembered childhood dream.

"Let's go," said Hermit, setting off briskly.

"Tell me," said Six-Toes, slipping on the tiled surface as he walked beside him, "how do you know when the night's about to start?"

"From the clock," Hermit answered. "It's one of the heavenly bodies. At present it's up above us on the right, that disc with the black zigzags on it."

Six-Toes looked up at the familiar detail of the vault of heaven, to which he had never previously paid any particular attention.

"When some of those black lines reach a certain position, which I'll tell you about later, the light goes out," said Hermit. "It's going to happen any second now. Count to ten."

"One, two—" Six-Toes began, and suddenly it was dark.

"Don't fall behind," said Hermit, "or you'll get lost."

He needn't have said it, since Six-Toes was almost treading on his heels. The only remaining source of light in the universe was the yellow beam that slanted from behind the green gates of Shop Number One. The place towards which Hermit and Six-Toes were heading was quite close to the gates, but Hermit assured him that it was the safest.

All they could see now was a distant strip of yellow under the gates and a few tiles around them. Six-Toes fell into a strange state, feeling as though the darkness was crushing in on them in the same way that the crowd had squeezed them only a while before. There was danger on every side, and Six-Toes sensed it acutely like a cold draft blowing from all sides at once. When his fear became too strong for him to go on, he raised his gaze from the tiles to the strip of yellow light under the gates and then remembered the community, which had looked almost like the same from a distance. He felt as though they were walking into a kingdom inhabited by fire-spirits, and he was just about to tell Hermit about it, when Hermit suddenly stopped and raised his arm.

"Quiet," he said. "Rats. Over to our right."

There was nowhere to run. The expanse of tiles extended into the distance on every side, and the strip of light was still too far ahead. Hermit turned to the right and stood in a strange pose, telling Six-Toes to hide behind him. Six-Toes did so only too willingly, and with quite remarkable speed.

At first he couldn't make out anything at all, and then in the darkness he sensed, rather than saw, the rapid movement of a large, agile body. It halted precisely at the limit of his vision.

"It's waiting," Hermit said softly, "for us to go on. We only have to take a single step, and it will fling itself at us."

"Aha, I'll fling myself, all right" said the rat, emerging from the darkness. "Like a bundle of malice and fury. Like a creature truly begotten of the night."

"Oh," Hermit gasped, "One-Eye. And I thought we'd really had it. Let me introduce you."

Six-Toes stared suspiciously into the intelligent conical face with the long moustaches and two round black beads for eyes.

"One-Eye," said the rat in self-introduction and waved his indecently naked tail.

"Six-Toes," said Six-Toes in reply, and asked: "Why do they call you One-Eye, when you have two perfectly good eyes?"

"That's because my third eye has been opened," One-Eye answered, "and I've only one third eye. In a certain sense anyone whose third eye is open is one-eyed."

"What's a—" Six-Toes began, but Hermit cut him off before he could finish.

"Why don't we take a stroll," he suggested gallantly, "over to those boxes? The night road is wearisome without a companion to talk to."

Six-Toes was deeply offended.

"By all means," One-Eye agreed, turning his back on Six-Toes (who was now presented with his first clear view of the huge muscular body), and stepping out beside Hermit, who had to walk very fast to keep up with him. Six-Toes ran along behind, looking at One-Eye's feet and the muscles rippling under his skin, worrying how this encounter might have ended had One-Eye not been an acquaintance of Hermit's, and trying very hard not to tread on the rat's tail. Their conversation rapidly began to sound like the continuation of a previous discussion; they were obviously old friends.

"Freedom! My God, what's that?" One-Eye asked, laughing. "Is that running around the combine, confused and alone, after you've just dodged the knife again for the tenth time, or the hundredth? Is that what freedom is?"

"There you go substituting one thing for another again," answered Hermit. "That's nothing but the search for freedom. I shall never accept that infernal picture—the world you believe in. It's all because you feel like an alien in this universe that was created for us."

"The rats may believe it was created for us—I don't say that because I agree with them. You're right, of course, but not completely right—and not about the most important thing. You say this universe was created for you? No, it was created because of you, but not for you. Do you understand?"

Hermit lowered his head and walked on in silence.

"All right then," said One-Eye, "it's time for me to say goodbye. I was expecting you to turn up a bit later, but we've met anyway. I'm going away tomorrow."

"Where to?"

"Beyond the bounds of everything that can be spoken of. One of the old burrows led me to an empty concrete pipe that runs so far I couldn't even imagine how long it is. I met some rats there, and they say that the pipe goes on deeper and deeper, until it emerges into another universe down below us. There are only male gods and they all wear the same green clothing. They perform complicated rituals around immense idols which stand in gigantic shafts."

One-Eye slowed his pace.

"I turn right here," he said. "They say the food there is indescribable. And this entire universe would fit into one single shaft down there. Why don't you come along with me?"

"No," replied Hermit, "our way does not lie downwards."

For the first time since the conversation began, he seemed to recall the existence of Six-Toes.

"In that case," said One-Eye, "I wish you success on your journey, wherever it may take you. Farewell."

One-Eye nodded to Six-Toes and disappeared into the darkness as suddenly as he had emerged.

Hermit and Six-Toes walked the rest of the way in silence. As they came closer to the boxes, they had to pick their way across all the heaps of shavings. At long last they reached their goal, a declivity in the shavings with a heap of soft rags lying in it, gently illuminated by the light from beneath the gates of Shop Number One. Close by the wall stood a huge ribbed structure which Hermit said had once emitted such intense heat that he couldn't even approach it. He was rummaging about in the rags to make himself comfortable for the night, and Six-Toes decided not to pester him with questions, especially since he felt sleepy himself. He burrowed into the rags and fell into oblivion.

He was woken by a distant scraping, the sound of steel grinding on wood, and screams of such utter hopelessness that he rushed over to Hermit immediately: "What is that?"

"Your world's passing through its Decisive Stage," Hermit answered.

"What?"

"Death has come," Hermit said simply. He turned away, pulled a scrap of rag over himself, and fell asleep.

V

When he woke, Hermit glanced over at Six-Toes trembling in the corner, his eyes red from crying, then cleared his throat and began rummaging in the rags. Soon he had taken out ten identical iron objects that looked like sections cut from a thick six-sided pipe.

"Take a look at these," he said to Six-Toes.

"What are they?" Six-Toes asked.

"The gods call them nuts."

Six-Toes seemed on the point of asking another question, but instead he waved his hand in the air and burst into tears again.

"What in the world's the matter?" asked Hermit.

"They're all dead," Six-Toes babbled. "Every last one of them—"

"What of it?" said Hermit. "You'll die too. And you can be sure you'll be dead for just as long as they will."

"Yes, but I feel sorry for them."

"Sorry for who? The Old Mothers?

"Remember how they threw us over the wall?" Six-Toes asked. "When everybody was ordered to keep his eyes shut? I waved to them, and somebody waved back, and when I think that he's dead too. . . . And whatever made him do that has died with him. . . ."

"Yes," said Hermit, "that really is very sad."

There was silence, broken only by the mechanical sounds behind the green gates through which Six-Toes' former home had glided.

"Tell me," Six-Toes asked, his voice hoarse from crying, "what happens after we die?"

"It's hard to say," answered Hermit. "I've had many visions about it, but I don't know how much I can trust them."

"Tell me about them, will you?"

"As a rule, after death we are plunged into Hell. I've counted at least fifty variations on what happens. Sometimes the dead are divided up and cooked in immense frying pans. Sometimes they are roasted whole in an iron-walled room with a glass door where there are roaring blue flames or white-hot metal pillars radiating intense heat. Sometimes we are boiled in huge vessels of various colors, and, sometimes, quite the opposite, we are frozen in a lump of ice. All in all, not a very comforting prospect."

"But who does all that?"

"Who? The gods, of course."

"But why?"

"That's simple, we happen to be their food."

Six-Toes shuddered and then stared down intently at his own trembling knees.

"They like the legs best of all," Hermit observed. "And the arms too. It's your arms I wanted to talk to you about. Hold them out."

Six-Toes held out his arms in front of him: skinny and powerless, they were a pitiful sight.

"There was a time when we used them to fly," said Hermit, "but then everything changed."

"What does 'to fly' mean?"

"Nobody knows exactly. The only thing we do know is that you need strong arms for it. A lot stronger than yours or even mine. What I want to do now is teach you an exercise to do. Get two of the nuts."

Six-Toes struggled to drag over two of the stupendously heavy objects to Hermit's feet.

"Right. Now stick the ends of your arms into the holes."

Six-Toes did that too.

"Now lift the nuts up and down, up and down. . . . That's right."

After a minute of this Six-Toes was so exhausted he couldn't keep lifting the nuts no matter how hard he tried.

"I can't," he said, dropping his arms so the nuts crashed down on to the floor.

"Now watch how I do it," said Hermit, putting five nuts on the end of each arm. He held his arms out to the side for several minutes and didn't seem to get tired at all.

"How about that?"

"That's fantastic," sighed Six-Toes, "but why are you just holding them still?"

"With this exercise there's a difficulty that arises at a certain point. Later on you'll understand what I mean."

"Are you sure you can learn to fly this way?"

"No, I'm not sure. On the contrary, I suspect it's quite pointless."

"Then what's it good for? If you know yourself that it's quite pointless?"

"How can I put it? I know all sorts of other things apart from this, and one of them is that if you're in the dark and you glimpse even the slightest glimmering of light, you have to move towards it. You don't stop to ponder whether there's any point to it. Maybe there really isn't any point. But there's certainly no point in just sitting there in the dark. Do you understand?"

Six-Toes didn't answer.

"We only stay alive as long as we have hope," said Hermit. "And if you lose hope, you mustn't ever let yourself realize it. Then something just might change. But you should never seriously rely on that."

Six-Toes was exasperated: "That's all wonderful, but what does it really mean?"

"What it really means for you is that every day you're going to exercise with these nuts until you can do what I do."

"Is that the only thing I can do?"

"There are alternatives; for instance, you can prepare for the Decisive Stage. But you'll have to do that on your own."

VI

"Listen, Hermit, you know everything there is to know. Tell me what love is."

"Strange, where did you hear that word?"

"When they drove me out of the community, they asked

me if I loved the things that should be loved. I said I didn't know."

"I doubt if I can explain it to you. You can only learn by example. Imagine you've fallen into water and you're drowning. Can you imagine that?"

"Uhu!"

"And now imagine that just for a second you're able to lift your head above water, see the light, take a gulp of air, and feel your hands touch something, so you grab hold and cling to it. So, if you can imagine that all of your life you are drowning—and that's certainly nothing but the truth—then love is what helps you keep your head above water."

"Do you mean love for the things that should be loved?"

"That's not important. Although, generally speaking, you can love the things that should be loved even when you've gone under. It can be anything at all. What does it matter what you grab hold of, as long as it keeps you afloat? The worst thing is if it turns out to be someone else—he can always pull his hand away. If you want to keep it simple, love is the reason why everyone is where they are. Except maybe the dead . . . although—"

"I don't think I've ever loved anyone," Six-Toes broke in.

"No, it's happened to you too. Remember how you sat there crying your eyes out, thinking about the person who waved back to you when they were throwing us over the wall? That was love. You don't know why he did it. Maybe he just thought he was mocking you a bit more subtly than all the rest—that's probably what it was. That means you behaved very stupidly, but absolutely correctly. Love gives meaning to what we do, even though it actually has no meaning."

"So you mean that love deceives us? Is it something like a dream?"

"No. Love is something like love, and a dream is a dream. Everything that you do, you do out of nothing but love. Otherwise you would just sit on the ground and howl in terror. Or in disgust."

"But the reason lots of people do what they do has nothing to do with love."

"Nonsense. Those people don't do anything at all."

"Is there anything you love, Hermit?"

"Yes."

"What is it?"

"I don't know. Something that comes to me sometimes. Sometimes it's some kind of thought, sometimes the nuts, sometimes a dream. The important thing is that I always recognize it, whatever form it takes, and I greet it as best I can."

"How?"

"By becoming calm."

"Does that mean you're worried all the rest of the time?"

"No, I'm always calm. It's just that this calm is the very best thing I have in me, and when this thing I love comes to me, I offer it my calmness."

"And what do you think is best about me?"

"About you? Probably when you sit there quietly somewhere in a corner."

"Really?"

"I don't know. If you really want to, you can work out what the best thing in you is by thinking what it is you offer when you feel love. What did you feel, when you were thinking about the person who waved to you?"

"Sadness."

"Well, that means the best thing in you is your sadness, and that's how you'll always greet anything you love."

Hermit glanced round and listened to something.

"Do you want to take a look at the gods?" he asked suddenly.

"Not right now, please," Six-Toes answered in panic.

"Don't be afraid. They're very stupid—not at all frightening. Just take a look. There they are, over there."

Two vast beings were walking quickly along the path by the conveyor belt, their figures so huge that their heads were lost in the semi-darkness under the ceiling. Walking behind them came another similar form, only shorter and fatter, carrying a vessel in the shape of a truncated cone, with the narrow end towards the ground. The first two stopped not far from where Hermit and Six-Toes were sitting and began making low growling sounds—Six-Toes guessed that they were talking—and the third being went over to the wall, set the vessel on the floor, plunged a pole with bristles on it into the vessel and then moved it across the dirty-grey wall, leaving a fresh dirty-grey line. There was a strange smell.

"Listen," Six-Toes said in a scarcely audible whisper, "you said you know their language. What are they saying?"

"These two? Just a second. The first is saying, 'I want a skinful.' And the other's saying, 'You just keep away from Masha from now on'."

"What's a Masha?"

"It's a region of the world."

"Ah. . . . And what does the first one want to fill his skin with?"

"Masha, probably," Hermit replied after a pause for thought.

"But how can he fit a whole part of the world inside him?"

"Well, they are gods, after all."

"And what's that one, the fat one, saying?"

"She's not saying anything, she's singing. About how when she dies she wants to become a willow tree. Actually, that's my favorite song of the gods—it's a pity I don't know what a willow tree is."

"Do the gods die, then?"

"Sure they do. That's what they're busy with most of the time."

The two tall beings walked on. "How magnificent!" Six-Toes thought in awe. The heavy footfalls of the gods and their low voices died away and there was silence. A draft swirled the dust along above the tiled surface of the floor and Six-Toes felt as though he was looking down from some unimaginably high mountain at an expanse of strange rocky desert where the same things happen again and again for millions and milions of years: the wind rushes over the surface of the land, bearing along the remnants of lives that once belonged to somebody, and from a distance they look just like pieces of straw, scraps of paper, or woodshavings. "There'll come a time," Six-Toes thought, "when someone else will look down from here and think about me, without even knowing that he is thinking about me. Just as I'm thinking about someone who felt the same as me, but God only knows when that was. In every day there is a point which binds it to the past and the future. What a sad place this world is. . . ."

"And yet there is something in it that justifies even the very saddest life," Hermit said suddenly.

"To die and be a willow tree," the fat goddess was crooning softly beside her bucket of paint. Six-Toes lowered his head onto his arm in sadness, but Hermit remained absolutely calm, staring off into the emptiness, as though he was gazing over thousands of invisible heads.

VII

While Six-Toes spent his time exercising with the nuts, dozens of worlds departed into Shop Number One. There were creaking and banging sounds behind the green gates as something happened there, and Six-Toes broke into a cold sweat and began trembling at the thought of what it might be, but this lent him strength. His arms had grown noticeably longer and stronger, and now they were just like Hermit's, but so far there had been no other result. The only thing Hermit knew was that you used your arms to fly, but what "flying" meant wasn't clear. Hermit believed it was some special method of instantaneous displacement in space: you had to imagine the place you wanted to get to, and then mentally command your arms to take your entire body there. He spent days in meditation, trying to move himself just a few steps, but nothing came of it.

"Probably," he said to Six-Toes, "our arms are not strong enough yet. We'll just have to carry on exercising."

One day, when Hermit and Six-Toes, seated on their bundle of rags among the boxes, were contemplating the essence of things, something very unpleasant happened. Darkness suddenly fell, and when Six-Toes opened his eyes he saw the unshaven face of one of the gods suspended in space in front of him.

"Well, just look where they've got to!" said the face, and then a pair of immense dirty hands seized Hermit and Six-Toes, dragged them out from behind the boxes, carried them with unbelievable speed across the immense space, and threw them into one of the worlds that was already close to Shop Number One. At first Hermit and Six-Toes took this all calmly, even with a certain irony. They settled in beside the Wall of the World and began making their soul-sanctuaries, but then the god unexpectedly came back, dragged Six-Toes out, and looked him over carefully, smacking his lips in amazement. Then he tied a piece of sticky blue ribbon round his leg and threw him back. A few minutes later several of the gods arrived together. They lifted Six-Toes out and took turns looking at him with delighted expressions on their faces.

"I don't like this," said Hermit, when the gods finally went away. "It looks bad."

"I think so too," said Six-Toes, scared out of his wits. "Maybe I should take this crap off?"

He pointed to the blue ribbon wrapped around his leg.

"Better not take it off just yet," said Hermit.

For a while there was gloomy silence, then Six-Toes said: "It's all because of my six toes. Let's get out of here fast, they'll be looking for us again. They know about the boxes, but there must somewhere else we can hide?"

Hermit became even more morose, and instead of answering the question, he suggested they take a walk to the local community to unwind. But as it happened, an entire deputation was already making its way towards them from the distant twin-troughs. Judging from the fact that when they were still twenty paces away from them, the members of the delegation fell to the ground and began crawling, their intentions had to be serious. Hermit ordered Six-Toes to retreat, while he went ahead to find out what was the matter. When he came back, he said:

"I've really never seen anything like this before. They're obviously very pious. At least, they saw you associating with the gods and now they think you're the Messiah and I'm your disciple, or something like that."

"So what's going to happen now? What do they want?"

"They want us to visit them. They say some path or other has been made straight, something or other has been bound fast, and other things like that. And most important of all, it's exactly what they have in their scriptures. I don't understand a thing, but I think we should probably go along."

"Let's go, then," said Six-Toes with an indifferent shrug of his shoulders. He felt dark presentiments.

On the way it cost Hermit a lot of effort to rebuff their repeated and persistent attempts to carry him on their shoulders. Nobody dared so much as lift their eyes to Six-Toes, much less approach him, and he walked along at the center of a large circle of emptiness.

When they arrived they seated Six-Toes on a tall pile of straw, while Hermit remained at its foot and fell into conversation with the local spiritual authorities, about twenty of them, easily distinguished by their fat, flabby faces. He blessed them and clambered up the heap of straw to Six-Toes, who was now in such a bad mental state that he didn't even respond to Hermit's ritual bow, but everybody found that entirely natural anyway.

It turned out that they'd all been expecting the advent of the Messiah for a long time, because the approach of the Decisive Stage—which was called the Day of Condiment here, a clear indication that the local inhabitants had moments of serious insight—had been exercising their minds for ages, while the local spiritual authorities had become so gorged and idle that they answered every question put to them with a brief gesture of the head in the direction of the ceiling. And so the appearance of Six-Toes and his disciple had proved very timely indeed.

"They're waiting for a sermon," said Hermit.

"Well, spin them some kind of story, then," Six-Toes blurted out. "You know perfectly well I'm just plain stupid."

At the word stupid, his voice trembled, and it was clear to everyone that he was on the verge of tears.

"They're going to eat me, those gods," he said, "I can feel it."

"Come on, calm down," said Hermit. He turned to the crowd around the heap of straw and adopted a prayerful posture, turning his face to the heavens and raising his arms on high. "All of you below!" he shouted. "Soon you shall enter Hell. There all shall be roasted and the most sinful among you shall first be marinated in vinegar!"

A gasp of horror ran though the air above the crowd.

"But I, by the will of the gods and their emissary, my master, wish to teach you how to save yourselves. To do this you must conquer sin—but do you even know what sin is?"

The only answer was silence.

"Sin is excess weight. Your flesh is sinful, for because of it the gods strike you down. Why, do you think, the Decisive Stage . . . the Day of Judgment is fast approaching? It is because you are growing fat. For the thin shall be saved, but the fat shall not. Verily I say unto you: not a single bony and blue one shall be cast into the fire, but the fat and the pink shall all be there. But those who from this day forth until the very Day of Judgment shall fast, shall be born again. Oh, Lord! And now arise and sin no more!"

But no one stood up, they all lay there on the ground, staring in silence, some at Hermit waving his hands, some at the gulf of the ceiling above them. Many wept. The only ones who didn't seem impressed by Hermit's speech were the high priests.

"Why did you say that?" Six-Toes whispered when Hermit lowered himself on to the straw beside him. "They believed you!"

"Well, was I lying?" answered Hermit. "If they lose a lot of weight, they'll be sent on a second feeding cycle, and then maybe on a third. We can't waste any more time on them, let's think about our own business."

VIII

Hermit spoke frequently with the community, teaching them how to make themselves appear as unappetizing as possible, and Six-Toes spent most of his time sitting on his mountain of straw and contemplating the nature of flight. He took almost no part in the discussions and only occasionally bestowed on the laymen who crept closer to him an absent-minded blessing. The former high priests, who had not the slightest intention of going hungry, gazed at him with hatred in their eyes, but there was nothing they could do, because different gods kept coming to their world, grabbing Six-Toes, looking at him closely and showing him to one another. On one occasion the world was even visited by a heavy-jowled old god with grey hair surrounded by a large retinue, to whom the other gods showed the utmost deference. When the old god picked him up, Six-Toes deliberately shat straight onto his cold trembling palm, after which he was rather roughly set back into his place.

At night, when everyone was asleep, he and Hermit carried on frantically training their arms—the less they believed that it would lead to anything, the greater the effort they applied. Their arms had grown so much that it was no longer possible to exercise with the pieces of iron Hermit had extracted from the food and water troughs when he dismantled them—the members of the community were still fasting and now looked almost transparent—because as soon they began waving their arms, their feet parted from the ground and they had to stop. This was the difficulty that Hermit had once warned Six-Toes about, but they found a way round it: Hermit knew how to strengthen his muscles by means of static exercises, and he taught Six-Toes how. The green gates were already visible beyond the Wall of the World, and Hermit had calculated that there were only ten eclipses left till the Day of Judgement. The gods didn't scare Six-Toes too much now, he'd grown used to their constant attention, accepting it with disdainful humility. His mental balance had been restored and, to amuse himself a little, he began giving dark, almost unintelligible sermons which shook his flock to the core. Once he recalled One-Eye's tale of the underground universe and in a burst of inspiration he described the preparation of the soup for a hundred and sixty demons dressed in green uniforms in such minute detail that by the end of it not only was he himself half-scared to death, but he had seriously alarmed Hermit into the bargain. Many members of the flock learned this sermon by heart, and it became known as "The Revelation of the Blue Ribbon"—this was Six-Toes' sacred title. After this even the former high priests stopped eating and spent hours at a time running round the half-ruined troughs, trying desperately to work off their fat.

Since Hermit and Six-Toes were both eating for two, Hermit had to invent a special dogma of impeccable infallibility, which put a swift end to any whispered murmurs of dissent.

But while Six-Toes rapidly regained his balance after the shock they had experienced, something seemed to be wrong with Hermit. As if Six-Toes' depression had been transferred to him, he became more withdrawn with every passing hour.

Once he said to Six-Toes: "You know, if we don't pull this off, I'm going into Shop Number One along with the rest of them."

Before Six-Toes could open his mouth to object, Hermit stopped him: "And since it's certain we won't pull it off, we can regard the whole thing as settled."

Six-Toes suddenly realized that what he had been about to say was quite pointless. He couldn't change someone else's mind, all he could do was express his own affection for Hermit, so whatever he might say the meaning would be the same. Earlier he probably wouldn't have been able to resist indulging in pointless chatter, but recently something in him had changed. He simply nodded, then moved away, and deliberately immersed himself in contemplation. Soon he came back and said: "I'll go with you."

"No," said Hermit, "you mustn't do that, no matter what. Now you know almost everything that I do, and you have to stay alive and take a disciple. Perhaps at least he will come close to learning how to fly."

"Do you want to leave me alone?" Six-Toes asked irritably. "With these cattle?"

He pointed to the members of the flock, who had stretched themselves out on the ground at the beginning of the prophets' conversation—identical exhausted and trembling bodies covered the ground for almost as far as they could see.

Hermit looked down at his friend's feet with a chuckle. "Tell me, do you remember what you were like before we met?"

Six-Toes thought for a moment and felt embarrassed. "No," he said, "I don't remember. Honestly, I don't remember."

"All right," said Hermit, "you do whatever you think best."

And that was the end of the conversation.

The days remaining until the end flew by. One morning, when the flock had only just opened its eyes, Hermit and Six-Toes noticed that the green gates, which yesterday had seemed far away, were already towering up over the Wall of the World. They glanced at each other and Hermit said: "Today we'll make our last attempt. The last attempt, because tomorrow there won't be anyone left to make another one. We'll go over to the Wall of the World so that this hubbub can't distract us, and we'll try to get from there to the dome of the troughs. If we don't manage it, then we can say our farewells to the world."

"How is that done?" Six-Toes asked by force of habit.

Hermit stared at him in astonishment.

"How should I know how it's done?" he said.

Everyone was told that the prophets were going to communicate with the gods. Soon Hermit and Six-Toes found themselves beside the Wall of the World and they sat down with their backs against it.

"Remember," said Hermit, "you have to imagine that you're already there, and then. . . ."

Six-Toes closed his eyes, focused all his attention on his arms and began thinking about the rubber hose-pipe that hung down to the roof of the troughs. Gradually he fell into a trance, and he had the distinct feeling that the hose-pipe was right beside him and he could reach out his hand to touch it. On previous occasions Six-Toes had always been in a hurry to open his eyes, and he'd always found himself still sitting in the same place, but this time he decided to try something new. "If I slowly bring my arms together," he thought, "so that they wrap round the hose, what then?" Cautiously, trying hard to maintain the certainty he had attained that the hose-pipe was close beside him, he began to move his arms towards each other. And when they closed together on the hose-pipe, where previously there had been only empty space, he began screeching at the top of his voice: "I did it! I did it!"

He opened his eyes.

"Quiet, you fool," said Hermit, who was standing in front of him, and whose leg he was clutching. "Look."

Six-Toes leapt to his feet and looked around. The gates of Shop Number One stood wide open, towering over them as they glided slowly past.

"We've arrived. Let's walk back."

On the way back they didn't say a word. The belt of the conveyor was moving at the same speed as Hermit and Six-Toes were walking, but in the opposite direction, so the entrance to Shop Number One was always there beside them. And when they reached their places of honor beside the two troughs, the entrance moved over and past them.

Hermit called one of the flock to him.

"Listen," he said, "only keep calm! Go and tell the others

that the Day of Judgment has arrived. Do you see how dark the sky has grown?"

"And what shall we do now?" the other asked hopefully.

"Everyone must sit on the ground and do this," said Hermit, covering his eyes with his hands. "And don't try to peep, or we can't guarantee anything. And be sure to keep quiet."

At first even so there was a great hubbub, but it quickly died away and everyone sat on the ground as Hermit had said.

"Well, then," said Six-Toes, "shall we say our goodbyes to the world?"

"Yes," answered Hermit. "You go first."

Six-Toes stood up, glanced around him, sighed, and sat back down again.

"That's it?" Hermit asked.

Six-Toes nodded.

"Now it's my turn," said Hermit, rising to his feet. He threw back his head and shouted with all his might: "Goodbye, world!"

IX

"Listen to that one cackle," said a voice of thunder. "Which one was it? That one clucking over there?"

"No," said a different voice, "the one beside him."

Two huge faces appeared above the Wall of the World. The gods.

"What a bunch of crap," said the first face with disappointment. "I don't see what we can do with this lot. Half-dead already, every one of them."

An immense arm clad in a blood-spattered white sleeve coated in down reached out at tremendous speed across the world to touch the twin troughs.

"Semyon, fuck you, are you blind? Their feed system's broken!"

"There wasn't anything wrong with it before," a deep bass

voice replied. "I checked everything at the beginning of the month. What now, are we going to slaughter them?"

"No. Turn the conveyor on and move up another container, and make sure you get that feed system fixed tomorrow. It's a miracle they haven't all croaked. . . ."

"Okay, okay."

"What about this one, with the six toes, do you want both feet?"

"Yeah, cut 'em both off."

"I wanted one for myself."

Hermit turned to Six-Toes, who was listening carefully but not understanding very much.

"Listen," he said, "it seems they want to—"

At that very moment that white arm hurtled across the sky once again and clutched Six-Toes.

Six-Toes didn't hear what Hermit was trying to tell him. The huge hand grabbed him and plucked him from the ground, and then he was facing a large chest with a fountain pen sticking out of its pocket, a shirt-collar and, finally, a pair of huge bulging eyes that stared fixedly at him.

"Hey, look at the wings on him! Like an eagle," said the giant mouth with its yellow, irregular teeth.

Six-Toes had long ago grown used to being handled by the gods, but this time the hands that held him gave off a strange, frightening vibration. All he could make out of the conversation was that they were talking about his arms or about his legs, but then suddenly he heard Hermit shouting up at him like a madman.

"Six-Toes, run for it! Peck him in the face!"

For the first time ever, he heard despair in Hermit's voice, and Six-Toes felt scared, so scared that his every move acquired a somnambulistic precision. He pecked with all his might at the goggling eyes and at the same time he began beating at the god's sweaty face from both sides with incredibly fast movements.

There was a roar so loud that Six-Toes felt it not as a sound, but as pressure against the entire surface of his body. The god's fingers released their grip and a moment later Six-Toes realized that he was up under the ceiling, hanging in the air without any support. At first he couldn't understand what was happening, then he saw that out of sheer repetition he was still flapping his arms to and fro and this was what was holding him up. From up here he could see the true shape of Shop Number One: it was a section of the conveyor, walled in on both sides, runnning beside a long wooden table covered in red and brown blotches, scattered with down and feathers and piles of clear plastic bags. The world in which Hermit still remained was no more than an octagonal container filled with tiny, motionless bodies. Six-Toes could not see Hermit, but he was certain that Hermit could see him.

"Hey," he shouted, flying round in circles just under the ceiling. "Hermit! Come up here, quick! Flap your arms as fast as you can!"

There was a movement down below and Hermit's form gradually grew larger as it came nearer, until he appeared there beside him. He circled a few times after Six-Toes and then shouted: "Let's land over there!"

When Six-Toes flew up to the square patch of dim, milky light, dissected by a narrow cross, Hermit was already sitting on the window sill.

"The wall," he said when Six-Toes landed beside him, "the wall, it shines."

Outwardly Hermit appeared calm but Six-Toes knew him well enough to see that he was shaken by what was happening. Six-Toes felt the same. Suddenly the realization hit him. "Listen," he shouted, "that was flying! We were flying!"

Hermit nodded. "I realized that already," he said. "The truth's so simple it could make you weep."

Meanwhile the disorderly fluttering movement of the figures below had settled down somewhat, and they could see two gods in white coats restraining their companion, who was holding his hand to his face.

"That bastard! He's put my eye out!" the third god was yelling. "The bastard!"

"What's a bastard?" Six-Toes asked.

"It's a way of invoking one of the elemental forces," Hermit answered. "The word doesn't have any real meaning of its own."

"What elemental force is he invoking?" Six-Toes asked.

"We'll soon see," Hermit said.

While Hermit was speaking, the god shrugged off the hands that were holding him back, dashed across to the wall, wrenched down the red fire extinguisher, and hurled it at them where they sat on the window sill. He did it all so quickly that no one could stop him, and Hermit and Six-Toes barely managed to fly off in opposite directions.

There was a ringing sound, followed by a clang. The fire extinguisher broke the window and then disappeared, and a gust of fresh air swept past them, which immediately made clear what a terrible stench there had been before. An intense bright light flooded in.

"Fly for it," Hermit shrieked, instantly losing his former imperturbability. "Move it! Go!"

He flew away from the window, picked up speed, turned back, folded his wings, and disappeared into the beam of hot yellow light pouring in through the hole in the painted glass together with the wind and the new, unfamiliar sounds.

Six-Toes circled, picking up speed. Down below he caught one last glimpse of the octagonal container, the table awash with blood, and the gods waving their arms in the air; then he folded in his wings and whistled through the gap in the window.

For a second he was blinded by the brightness of the light, and then his eyes adjusted. Ahead and above, he caught sight of a circle of yellow-white light too bright to look at even out of the corner of his eye. Higher still in the sky was the black speck that was Hermit. He circled so that Six-Toes could catch up with him, and soon they were flying side by side.

Six-Toes looked around. Far below them was a huge, ugly,

grey building with only a few windows, all painted over. One was broken. The colors of everything around it were so pure and bright that Six-Toes had to look up to stop himself from going out of his mind.

Flying was very easy; it required no more effort than walking. They climbed higher and higher, and soon everything below them was no more than a pattern of colored squares and blotches.

Six-Toes turned his head to look at Hermit.

"Where are we going?" he shouted

"To the South," Hermit replied briefly.

"What's that?" Six-Toes asked.

"I don't know," answered Hermit, "but it's that way."

He gestured with his wing in the direction of the huge glowing circle; only its color resembled what they had once called the lights of heaven.

THE LIFE
AND ADVENTURES
OF
SHED NUMBER XII

IN THE BEGINNING WAS THE word, and maybe not even just one, but what could he know about that? What he discovered at his point of origin was a stack of planks on wet grass, smelling of fresh resin and soaking up the sun with their yellow surfaces: he found nails in a plywood box, hammers, saws, and so forth—but visualizing all this, he observed that he was thinking the picture into existence rather than just seeing it. Only later did a weak sense of self emerge, when the bicycles already stood inside him and three shelves one above the other covered his right wall. He wasn't really Number XII then; he was merely a new configuration of the stack of planks. But those were the times that had left the most pure and enduring impression. All around lay the wide incomprehensible world, and it seemed as though he had merely interrupted his journey through it, making a halt here, at this spot, for a while.

Certainly the spot could have been better—out behind the low five-storey prefabs, alongside the vegetable gardens and the garbage dump. But why feel upset about something like that? He wasn't going to spend his entire life here, after all. Of course, if he'd really thought about it, he would have been forced to admit that that was precisely what he was going to do—that's the way it is for sheds—but the charm of life's earliest beginnings consists in the absence of such thoughts. He simply stood there in the sunshine, rejoicing in the wind whistling through his cracks if it blew from the woods, or falling into a slight depression if it blew in from over the dump. The depression passed as soon as the wind changed direction, without leaving any long-term effect on a soul that was still only partially formed.

One day he was approached by a man naked to the waist in a pair of red tracksuit pants, holding a brush and a huge can of paint. The shed was already beginning to recognize this man, who was different from all the other people because he could get inside, to the bicycles and the shelves. He stopped by the wall, dipped the brush into the can, and traced a bright crimson line on the planks. An hour later the hut was crimson all over. This was the first real landmark in his memory—everything that came before it was still cloaked in a sense of distant and unreal happiness.

The night after the painting (when he had been given his Roman numeral, his name—the other sheds around him all had ordinary numbers), he held up his tar-papered roof to the moon as he dried. "Where am I?" he thought. "Who am I?"

Above him was the dark sky and inside him stood the brand-new bicycles. A beam of light from the lamp in the yard shone on them through a crack, and the bells on their handlebars gleamed and twinkled more mysteriously than the stars. Higher up, a plastic hoop hung on the wall, and with the very thinnest of his planks Number XII recognized it as a symbol of the eternal riddle of creation which was also represented—so very wonderfully—in his own soul. On the shelves lay all sorts of stupid trifles that lent variety and uniqueness to his inner world. Dill and scented herbs hung drying on a thread stretched from one wall to another, reminding him of something that never ever happens to sheds—but since they reminded him of it anyway, sometimes it seemed that he once must have been not a mere shed, but a dacha, or at the very least a garage.

He became aware of himself, and realized that what he was

aware of, that is himself, was made up of numerous small individual features: of the unearthly personalities of machines for conquering distance, which smelled of rubber and steel; of the mystical introspection of the self-enclosed hoop; of the squeaking in the souls of the small items, such as the nails and nuts which were scattered along the shelves; and of other things. Within each of these existences there was an infinity of subtle variation, but still for him each was linked with one important thing, some decisive feeling—and fusing together, these feelings gave rise to a new unity, defined in space by the freshly painted planks, but not actually limited by anything. That was him, Number XII, and above his head the moon was his equal as it rushed through the mist and the clouds. . . . That night was when his life really began.

Soon Number XII realized that he liked most of all the sensation which was derived from or transmitted by the bicycles. Sometimes on a hot summer day, when the world around him grew quiet, he would secretly identify himself in turn with the "Sputnik" and the folding "Kama" and experience two different kinds of happiness.

In this state he might easily find himself forty miles away from his real location, perhaps rolling across a deserted bridge over a canal bounded by concrete banks, or along the violet border of the sun-baked highway, turning into the tunnels formed by the high bushes lining a narrow dirt track and then hurtling along it until he emerged onto another road leading to the forest, through the forest, through the open fields, straight up into the orange sky above the horizon: he could probably have carried on riding along the road till the end of his life, but he didn't want to, because what brought him happiness was the possibility itself. He might find himself in the city, in some yard where long stems grew out of the pavement cracks, and spend the evening there—in fact he could do almost anything.

When he tried to share some of his experiences with the occult-minded garage that stood beside him, the answer he received was that in fact there is only one higher happiness: the ecstatic union with the archetypal garage. So how could he tell his neighbor about two different kinds of perfect happiness, one of which folded away, while the other had three-speed gears?

"You mean I should try to feel like a garage too?" he asked one day.

"There is no other path," replied the garage. "Of course, you're not likely to succeed, but your chances are better than those of a kennel or a tobacco kiosk."

"And what if I like feeling like a bicycle?" asked Number XII, revealing his cherished secret.

"By all means, feel like one. I can't say you mustn't," said the garage. "For some of us feelings of the lower kind are the limit, and there's nothing to be done about it."

"What's that written in chalk on your side?" Number XII inquired.

"None of your business, you cheap piece of plywood shit," the garage replied with unexpected malice.

Of course, Number XII had only made the remark because he felt offended—who wouldn't by having his aspirations termed "lower"? After this incident there could be no question of associating with the garage, but Number XII didn't regret it. One morning the garage was demolished, and Number XII was left alone.

Actually, there were two other sheds quite close, to his left, but he tried not to think about them. Not because they were built differently and painted a dull, indefinite color—he could have reconciled himself with that. The problem was something else: on the ground floor of the five-storey prefab where Number XII's owners lived there was a big vegetable shop and these sheds served as its warehouses. They were used for storing carrots, potatoes, beets, and cucumbers, but the factor absolutely dominating every aspect of Number 13 and Number 14 was the pickled cabbage in two huge barrels covered with plastic. Number XII had often seen their great hollow bodies girt with steel hoops surrounded by a retinue of emaciated workmen who were rolling them out at an angle into the yard. At these times he felt afraid and he recalled one of the favorite maxims of the deceased garage, whom he often remembered with sadness, "There are some things in life which you must simply turn your back on as quickly as possible." And no sooner did he recall the maxim than he applied it. The dark and obscure life of his neighbors, their sour exhalations, and obtuse grip on life were a threat to Number XII: the very existence of these squat structures was enough to negate everything else. Every drop of brine in their barrels declared that Number XII's existence in the universe was entirely unnecessary: that, at least, that was how he interpreted the vibrations radiating from their consciousness of the world.

But the day came to an end, the light grew thick, Number XII was a bicycle rushing along a deserted highway and any memories of the horrors of the day seemed simply ridiculous.

It was the middle of the summer when the lock clanked, the hasp was thrown back, and two people entered Number XII: his owner and a woman. Number XII did not like her—somehow she reminded him of everything that he simply could not stand. Not that this impression sprang from the fact that she smelled of pickled cabbage—rather the opposite: it was the smell of pickled cabbage that conveyed some information about this woman, that somehow or other she was the very embodiment of the fermentation and the oppressive force of will to which Numbers 13 and 14 owed their present existence.

Number XII began to think, while the two people went on talking:

"Well, if we take down the shelves it'll do fine, just fine. . . ."

"This is a first-class shed," replied his owner, wheeling the bicycles outside. "No leaks or any other problems. And what a color!"

After wheeling out the bicycles and leaning them against the wall, he began untidily gathering together everything lying on the shelves. It was then that Number XII began to feel upset.

Of course, the bicycles had often disappeared for certain periods of time, and he knew how to use his memory to fill in the gap. Afterwards, when the bicycles were returned to their places, he was always amazed how inadequate the image his memory created was in comparison with the actual beauty that the bicycles simply radiated into space. Whenever they disappeared the bicycles always returned, and these short separations from the most important part of his own soul lent Number XII's life its unpredictable charm. But this time everything was different—the bicycles were being taken away forever.

He realized this from the unceremonious way that the man in the red pants was wreaking total devastation in him—nothing like this had ever happened before. The woman in the white coat had left long ago, but his owner was still rummaging around, raking tools into a bag, and taking down the old cans and patched inner tubes from the wall. Then a truck backed up to his door, and both bicycles dived obediently after the overfilled bags into its gaping tarpaulin maw.

Number XII was empty, and his door stood wide open.

Despite everything he continued to be himself. The souls of all that life had taken away continued to dwell in him, and although they had become shadows of themselves they still fused together to make him Number XII: but it now required all the willpower he could muster to maintain his individuality.

In the morning he noticed a change in himself. No longer interested in the world around him, his attention was focused exclusively on the past, moving in concentric rings of memory. He could explain this: when he left, his owner had forgotten the hoop, and now it was the only real part of his otherwise phantom soul, which was why Number XII felt like a closed circle. But he didn't have enough strength to feel really anything about this, or wonder if it was good or bad. A dreary, colorless yearning overlay every other feeling. A month passed like that.

One day workmen arrived, entered his defenseless open door, and in the space of a few minutes broke down the shelves. Number XII wasn't even fully aware of his new condition before his feelings overwhelmed him—which incidentally demonstrates that he still had enough vital energy left in him to experience fear.

They were rolling a barrel towards him across the yard. Towards him! In his great depths of nostalgic self-pity, he'd never dreamed anything could be worse than what had already happened—that this could be possible!

The barrel was a fearful sight. Huge and potbellied, it was very old, and its sides were impregnated with something hideous which gave out such a powerful stench that even the workers angling it along, who were certainly no strangers to the seamy side of life, turned their faces away and swore. And Number XII could also see something that the men couldn't: the barrel exuded an aura of cold attention as it viewed the world through the damp likeness of an eye. Number XII did not see them roll it inside and circle it around on the floor to set it at his very center—he had fainted.

Suffering maims. Two days passed before Number XII began to recover his thoughts and his feelings. Now he was different, and everything in him was different. At the very center of his soul, at the spot once occupied by the bicycles' windswept frames, there was pulsating repulsive living death, concentrated in the slow existence of the barrel and its equally slow thoughts, which were now Number XII's thoughts. He could feel the fermentation of the rotten brine, and the bubbles rose in him to burst on the surface, leaving holes in the layer of green mold. The swollen corpses of the cucumbers were shifted about by the gas, and the slime-impregnated boards strained against their rusty iron hoops inside him. All of it was him.

Numbers 13 and 14 no longer frightened him—on the contrary, he rapidly fell into a half-unconscious state of comradery with them. But the past had not totally disappeared; it had simply been pushed aside, squashed into a corner. Number XII's new life was a double one. On the one hand, he felt himself the equal

of Numbers 13 and 14, and yet on the other hand, buried somewhere deep inside him, there remained a sense of terrible injustice about what had happened to him. But his new existence's
center was located in the barrel, which emitted the constant gurgling and crackling sounds that had replaced the imagined
whooshing of tires over concrete.

Numbers 13 and 14 explained to him that all he had gone
through was just a normal life change that comes with age.

"The entry into the real world, with its real difficulties and
concerns, always involves certain difficulties," Number 13 would
say. "One's soul is occupied with entirely new problems."

And he would add some words of encouragement: "Never
mind, you'll get used to it. It's only hard at the beginning."

Number 14 was a shed with a rather philosophical turn of
mind. He often spoke of spiritual matters, and soon managed to
convince his new comrade that if the beautiful consisted of harmony ("That's for one," he would say) and inside you—objec-
tively speaking now—you had pickled cucumbers or pickled cabbage ("That's for two"), then the beauty of life consisted in
achieving harmony with the contents of the barrel and removing
all obstacles hindering that. An old dictionary of philosophical
terms had been wedged under his own barrel to keep it from
overflowing, and he often quoted from it. It helped him explain to
Number XII how he should live his life. Number 14 never did
feel complete confidence in the novice, however, sensing something in him that Number 14 no longer sensed in himself.

But gradually Number XII became genuinely resigned to the
situation. Sometimes he even experienced a certain inspiration,
an upsurge of the will to live this new life. But his new friends'
mistrust was well founded. On several occasions Number XII
caught glimpses of something forgotten, like a gleam of light
through a keyhole, and then he would be overwhelmed by a feeling of intense contempt for himself—and he simply hated the
other two.

Naturally, all of this was suppressed by the cucumber barrel's invincible worldview, and Number XII soon began to wonder what it was he'd been getting so upset about. He became simpler and the past gradually bothered him less because it was growing hard for him to keep up with the fleeting flashes of memory. More and more often the barrel seemed like a guarantee of stability and peace, like the ballast of a ship, and sometimes Number XII imagined himself like that, like a ship sailing out into tomorrow.

He began to feel the barrel's innate good nature, but only after he had finally opened his own soul to it. Now the cucumbers seemed almost like children to him.

Numbers 13 and 14 weren't bad comrades—and most importantly, they lent him support in his new existence. Sometimes in the evening the three of them would silently classify the objects of the world, imbuing everything around them with an all-embracing spirit of understanding, and when one of the new little huts that had recently been built nearby shuddered he would look at it and think: "How stupid, but never mind, it'll sow its wild oats and then it'll come to understand. . . ." He saw several such transformations take place before his own eyes, and each one served to confirm the correctness of his opinion yet again. He also experienced a feeling of hatred when anything unnecessary appeared in the world, but thank God, that didn't happen often. The days and the years passed, and it seemed that nothing would change again.

One summer evening, glancing around inside himself, Number XII came across an incomprehensible object, a plastic hoop draped with cobwebs. At first he couldn't make out what it was or what it might be for, and then suddenly he recalled that there were so many things that once used to be connected with this item. The barrel inside him was dozing, and some other part of him cautiously pulled in the threads of memory, but all of them were broken and they led nowhere. But there was something once, wasn't there? Or was there? He concentrated and tried to understand what it was he couldn't remember, and for a moment he stopped feeling the barrel and was somehow separate from it.

At that very moment a bicycle entered the yard and for no reason at all the rider rang the bell on his handlebars twice. It was enough—Number XII remembered:

A bicycle. A highway. A sunset. A bridge over a river.

He remembered who he really was and at last became himself, really himself. Everything connected with the barrel dropped off like a dry scab. He suddenly smelt the repulsive stench of the brine and saw his comrades of yesterday, Numbers 13 and 14, for what they really were. But there was no time to think about all this, he had to hurry: he knew that if he didn't do what he had to do now, the hateful barrel would overpower him again and turn him into itself.

Meanwhile the barrel had woken up and realized that something was happening. Number XII felt the familiar current of cold obtuseness he'd been used to thinking was his own. The barrel was awake and starting to fill him—there was only one answer he could make.

Two electric wires ran under his eaves. While the barrel was still getting its bearings and working out exactly what was wrong, he did the only thing he could. He squeezed the wires together with all his might, using some new power born of despair. A moment later he was overwhelmed by the invincible force emanating from the cucumber barrel, and for a while he simply ceased to exist.

But the deed was done: torn from their insulation, the wires touched, and where they met a purplish-white flame sprang into life. A second later a fuse blew and the current disappeared from the wires, but a narrow ribbon of smoke was already snaking up the dry planking. Then more flames appeared, and meeting no resistance they began to spread and creep towards the roof.

Number XII came round after the first blow and realized that the barrel had decided to annihilate him totally. Compressing his entire being into one of the upper planks in his ceiling, he could feel that the barrel was not alone—it was being helped by Numbers 13 and 14, who were directing their thoughts at him from outside.

"Obviously," Number XII thought with a strange sense of detachment, "what they are doing now must seem to them like restraining a madman, or perhaps they see an enemy spy whose cunning pretence to be one of them has now been exposed—".

He never finished the thought, because at that moment the barrel threw all its rottenness against the boundaries of his existence with redoubled force. He withstood the blow, but realized that the next one would finish him, and he prepared to die. But time passed, and no new blow came. He expanded his boundaries a little and felt two things—first, the barrel's fear, as cold and sluggish as every sensation it manifested; and second, the flames blazing all around, which were already closing in on the ceiling plank animated by Number XII. The walls were ablaze, the tar-paper roof was weeping fiery tears, and the plastic bottles of sunflower oil were burning on the floor. Some of them were bursting, and the brine was boiling in the barrel, which for all its ponderous might was obviously dying. Number XII extended himself over to the section of the roof that was still left, and summoned up the memory of the day he was painted, and more importantly, of that night: he wanted to die with that thought. Beside him he saw Number 13 was already ablaze, and that was the last thing he noticed. Yet death still didn't come, and when his final splinter burst into flames, something quite unexpected happened.

The director of Vegetable Shop 17, the same woman who had visited Number XII with his owner, was walking home in a foul mood. That evening, at six o'clock, the shed where the oil and cucumbers were stored had suddenly caught fire. The spilled oil had spread the fire to the other sheds—in short, everything that could burn had burned. All that was left of hut Number XII were the keys, and huts Number 13 and 14 were now no more than a few scorched planks.

While the reports were being drawn up and the explanations were being made to the firemen, darkness had fallen, and now the director felt afraid as she walked along the empty road with the trees standing on each side like bandits. She stopped and looked back to make sure no one was following her. There didn't seem to be anyone there. She took a few more steps, then glanced round again, and she thought she could see something twinkling in the distance. Just in case, she went to the edge of the road and stood behind a tree. Staring intently into the darkness, she waited to see what would happen. At the most distant visible point of the road a bright spot came into view. "A motorcycle!" thought the director, pressing hard against the tree trunk. But there was no sound of an engine.

The bright spot moved closer, until she could see that it was not moving on the surface of the road but flying along above it. A moment later, and the spot of light was transformed into something totally unreal—a bicycle without a rider, flying at a height of ten or twelve feet. It was strangely made; it somehow looked as though it had been crudely nailed together out of planks. But strangest of all was that it glowed and flickered and changed color, sometimes turning transparent and then blazing with an unbearably intense brightness. Completely entranced, the director walked out into the middle of the road, and to her appearance the bicycle quite clearly responded. Reducing its height and speed, it turned a few circles in the air above the dazed woman's head. Then it rose higher and hung motionless before swinging round stiffly above the road like a weather vane. It hung there for another moment or two and then finally began to move, gathering speed at an incredible rate until it was no more than a bright dot in the sky. Then that disappeared as well.

When she recovered her senses, the director found herself sitting in the middle of the road. She stood up, shook herself off, completely forgetting. . . . But then, she's of no interest to us.

Vera Pavlovna's
Ninth Dream

*Here we see that solipsism, strictly thought through,
coincides with pure realism.*
—Ludwig Wittgenstein

PERESTROIKA ERUPTED INTO
the public lavatory on Tverskoy Boulevard from several directions at once. The clients began squatting in their cubicles
longer, reluctant to part with the new sense of boldness they discovered in their scraps of newspaper. The spring light illuminat-
ing the stony faces of the gays jostling in the small tiled entranceway brought the intimation of long-awaited freedom, distant, as
yet, but already certain: those sections of obscene monologues in
which the leaders of the Party and the government were coupled
with the Lord God grew louder; the water and the electricity
were cut off more often.

Nobody caught up in all of this could make any real sense of
his involvement—nobody, that is, except Vera, the cleaning lady
in the men's toilet, a being of indeterminate age, and entirely sex-
less like all the rest of her colleagues. The changes that had set in
came as something of a surprise to Vera as well, but only to the
extent of the precise date at which they began and the precise

form in which they manifested themselves, because she herself was their source and origin.

It all began on that afternoon when Vera thought for the first time, not of the meaning of existence, as she usually did, but of its mystery. This resulted in her dropping her rag into the bucket of murky, sudsy water and emitting a sound something like a rather quiet "ah." The thought was quite unexpected and unbearable, and most remarkable of all, quite unconnected with anything in her surroundings. It simply manifested itself in a head into which nobody had invited it, leading to the conclusion that the long years of spiritual endeavor spent in the search for meaning had been wasted—because meaning was itself concealed within mystery. Vera nonetheless somehow managed to calm herself down and go on washing the floor.

When ten minutes had passed and she had already worked her way across a substantial portion of the tiles, a new consideration suddenly occurred to her, which was that this same idea could well occur to other people engaged in intellectual activity, and must, in fact have occurred to them, especially the older and more experienced ones. Vera began figuring out which members of her circle that might be, and quickly reached the certain conclusion that she did not have to look very far and could talk about it with Manyasha, the cleaner from the toilet next door, which was just like this one, only for women.

Manyasha was a little older, a skinny woman also of indeterminate but decidedly advanced age. For some reason, perhaps beause Manyasha always wove her hair into a gray plait at the back of her head, the sight of her always reminded Vera of the phrase "Dostoyevsky's Petersburg." Manyasha was Vera's oldest friend: they often exchanged photocopies of Blavatskaya and Ramacharaka, whose real name, according to Manyasha, was Silberstein. They went to the *Illusion* cinema to see Fassbinder and Bergman, but they hardly ever spoke about serious matters. Manyasha's mentorship of Vera's intellectual life was exercised in a quite unobtrusive and tangential fashion, and Vera never really felt aware of it.

No sooner had Vera recalled Manyasha, than the small employees' door between the two toilets opened (they had separate entrances from the street) and Manyasha herself appeared. Vera immediately launched into a confused explanation of her problem, and Manyasha listened without interrupting.

"So it turns out," Vera was saying, "that the search for the meaning of life is itself the only meaning of life. No, that's not it, it turns out that knowledge of the mystery of life, as distinct from an understanding of its meaning, makes it possible to control existence, that is, actually to put an end to an old life and begin a new one. Once the mystery has been mastered, no problem remains with the meaning."

"That's not exactly right," Manyasha interrupted, after listening attentively for a long time. "Or more precisely, it is absolutely right in every respect except that you fail to take into account the nature of the human spirit. Do you seriously believe that if you discovered this mystery you could solve every problem that arises?"

"Of course. I'm sure of it. But how can I discover it?"

Manyasha thought for a second, then she seemed to come to some decision and said:

"There's a rule involved here. If someone knows this mystery and you ask them about it, then they have to reveal it to you."

"Then why doesn't anyone know it?"

"Why do you think that? Some people do know it, and the others, obviously, never think to ask. Have you, for instance, ever asked anybody?"

"Well, let's say that I'm asking you now," Vera replied quickly.

"Then put your hand on the floor," Manyasha said, "so that you will bear the full responsibility for what is about to happen."

"Couldn't we do it without any of this playacting?" Vera grumbled, leaning down to the floor and placing her palm on a cold, square tile.

"Well, then?"

Manyasha beckoned Vera to come closer, then she took her head in her hands, tilted it so that Vera's ear was directly opposite her mouth, and whispered briefly into it. At that very moment there was a loud booming sound outside the walls of the lavatory.

"What, is that all?" Vera asked, straightening up. Manyasha nodded. Vera laughed doubtfully. Manyasha shrugged, as if to say she wasn't the one that thought it up, so she wasn't to blame. Vera stopped laughing.

"You know," she said, "I always suspected something of the sort."

Manyasha laughed.

"They all say that."

"Well then," said Vera, "for a start I'll try something simple. For instance, make pictures appear on the walls here and have some music playing."

"I think you'll be able to manage that," Manyasha said, "but don't forget that your efforts might produce unexpected results, something that seems to be entirely unrelated to what you're trying to do. The connection will only become clear later."

"But what could happen?"

"You'll see that for yourself."

It was some time before she did see, several months in fact, during those repulsive November days when it might be snow your feet are plowing through or it might be water, and it might be mist hanging in the air or it might be steam obscuring the sight of blue militia caps and the crimson bruises of banners held aloft.

What happened was that several proletarians in a festive mood descended into the toilet bearing a large quantity of ideological equipment: immense paper carnations on long green poles and incantations on special plywood sheets. Having relieved themselves, they set their bicolored lances against the walls, fenced off the urinals with their sodden plywood placards (the upper one bore the incomprehensible inscription: "Ninth Pipe-Drawing Brigade") and settled down for a small picnic in the narrow space in front of the mirror and the washbasin. The smell of fortified wine rapidly overpowered the smell of urine and chlorine. At first there was laughter and conversation, then a sudden silence fell, broken by a coarse male voice:

"You pouring that on the floor deliberately, you fucker?"

"No, 'course not," an unconvincing tenor replied hastily, "it's not the usual kind of bottle, the neck's shorter. I was listening to what you were saying. Try it yourself, Grigory, my hand just automatically . . ."

There was the sound of a blow striking against something soft and voices raised in approving obscenity, and after that the picnic somehow came to a rapid conclusion and the voices withdrew, echoing hollowly on the staircase up to the boulevard before they finally disappeared. Vera plucked up the courage to glance out of her corner.

A young man with his face beaten to pulp was sitting in the middle of the floor, spitting out blood at regular intervals onto the tiles that were awash with fortified port wine. At the sight of Vera he took fright, leapt to his feet and ran out on to the street, leaving behind in the entranceway a damp, broken carnation and a small board bearing the inscription: "There is no alternative to the paradigm of Perestroika!" Vera had not the slightest idea of the meaning contained in these words, but from her long experience of life she was quite certain that something new had begun, though she could not really believe that she had started it. Just to be on the safe side she picked up the gigantic flower and the placard and carried them into her own small room, which was made out of the two end cubicles. The partition between them had been removed and there was just enough space for a bucket, a mop, and a chair, in which she was able to take an occasional nap.

After this incident everything went on in the same old way for a long time. After all, what can happen in a toilet? Life proceeded smoothly and predictably, only the number of empty bottles that arrived each day began to fall, and people became less friendly.

One day a group of people appeared in the toilet who were clearly not there to relieve themselves. They were dressed in identical denim suits and dark glasses and they brought a folding ruler and one of those special things on a tripod stand (Vera didn't know what it was called) that people on the street sometimes look through at a stick with special markings held by someone else. The visitors measured the doorway, carefully surveyed the entire premises, and left without making any use of their optical device. A few days later they appeared again, accompanied by a man in a brown rain coat, carrying a brown briefcase (Vera knew him, he was the head of all the toilets in the city). This time the group behaved in a very strange manner: they didn't discuss anything or measure anything, they just walked backwards and forwards, with their shoulders bumping against the backs of the workers relieving themselves into the urinals (what an uncertain place this world is!) occasionally halting to peer meditatively at something invisible to Vera and the other visitors. Whatever it was, it must have been quite beautiful—she could tell from the smiles on their faces and the remarkably romantic poses they assumed.

Vera could never have expressed her feelings in words, but she understood everything perfectly, and for a few moments there arose before her inner eye a vision of the picture that used to hang in her nursery school: "Comrades Kirov, Voroshilov, and Stalin at the Building of the White Sea Baltic Canal." Two days later Vera learned that she was now working in a cooperative.

Her duties, by and large, remained the same as before, but everything in her surroundings changed. Gradually, and yet rapidly, with no delays or stoppages, the place was repaired. First the pale Soviet tiles on the wall were replaced with large tiles bearing images of green flowers. Then the cubicles were remodeled, their walls were paneled with imitation walnut formica, the severe white porcelain bowls of triumphant socialism were replaced by festive pinkish-purple chalices, and a turnstile was installed at the entrance, just like in the subway, except that entrance cost ten kopecks, not five.

When these transformations were completed Vera was given a raise of an entire 100 rubles a month and issued with new work clothes: a red peaked cap and a black garment halfway between overalls and an overcoat. Everything, in fact, was just like in the subway, except that the buttonholes and cockade were not adorned with the letter "S," but with two crossed streams of gold forged in thin copper. The double cubicle, where previously she could at least take a nap, was now transformed into a closet for toilet paper, and there was no way she could even squeeze inside.

Vera now sat beside the turnstiles, in a special booth like the throne of the Martian Communists in the film *Aelita*, smiling and changing money. Her movements acquired a smooth joyful rhythm, just like a sales assistant in the Eliseev shop she saw once in her childhood and remembered for the rest of her life. Bright blonde, with a generous, womanly figure, the sales assistant was slicing salmon against the background of a fresco depicting a sun-drenched valley where a cool bunch of grapes hung just half a meter outside reality, and it was morning, and the radio was playing softly, and Vera was a little girl in a red cotton dress.

The money jingled merrily in the turnstiles—every day they took in one and a half or two sacks full of it. "I seem to remember," Vera thought vaguely, "that somewhere Freud compares excrement to gold. He was certainly no fool, that's for sure—Why do people hate him so much? And then, that Nabokov . . ." She became absorbed in her usual unhurried stream of thought, but most of the thoughts consisted of no more than beginnings which had not yet crept as far as their own ends before they were overtaken by others. Life was gradually getting better and better. Green velvet curtains had appeared at the doorway, so that any-one entering had to separate them with his shoulder, and on the wall by the door hung a picture that was bought from a bankrupt diner: in rather strange perspective it depicted a troika of white horses harnessed to a hay-filled sleigh in which three passengers were paying not the slightest attention to the pack of wolves galloping after them in earnest pursuit. There were two men dressed in unbuttoned fur jackets playing accordions, and a woman without an accordion (which made the accordion a sexual characteristic).

The only thing that bothered Vera was the distant rumbling or roaring that she sometimes heard beyond the walls of the toilet—she had no idea what could possibly make such a strange sound under ground, but then she decided it must be the subway and stopped worrying. The cabins were filled with the rustling of genuine toilet paper—a far cry indeed from the old days. Pieces of soap appeared on the sinks, and beside them hung the boxes of electrical hand dryers. In short, when one regular client told Vera that he visited the toilet as he would a theater, she was not surprised at the comparison, and not even particularly flattered.

The new boss was a young, ruddy-faced guy dressed in a denim jacket and dark glasses, but he only showed up very occasionally, and Vera gathered he had another two or three toilets to keep an eye on. In Vera's eyes he seemed a mysterious and extremely powerful individual, but one day something happened which made it clear he was by no means in control of everything. When he came in from the street the ruddy-faced young guy usually thrust aside the green velvet curtain with a short, powerful movement of his open hand, then his face appeared, with two black glass ellipses in place of eyes, followed by the sound of his high-pitched voice. This time everything came in reverse order— first Vera heard his high, challenging tenor ringing out on the staircase, answered condescendingly by a gruff bass, and then the curtains parted. But instead of the hand and the dark glasses, what appeared was a denim-clad back that wasn't so much hunched over as folded. Vera's boss came backing in, trying to explain something as he went, and striding in after him came a fat elderly gnome with a big red beard, wearing a red cap and a red foreign T-shirt, on which Vera read the words: WHAT I REALLY NEED IS LESS SHIT FROM YOU PEOPLE.

The gnome was tiny, but the way he carried himself made him look taller than everyone else in the place. Glancing quickly around the premises, he opened his briefcase, took out a bundle of seals and applied one of them to a sheet of paper hastily proffered by Vera's boss. Then he uttered some brief instruction, prodded the young guy with the dark glasses in the belly with his finger, chuckled, and left. Vera didn't even notice him go. He was standing opposite the mirror, and then he was gone, as though he'd just plunged into the open mouth of some special gnome subway. Following the disincarnation of the midget with the seals Vera's boss calmed down, grew a lot taller and spoke a few phrases to no one in particular, from which Vera gathered that the gnome really was a very big man; he ruled over all the toilets in Moscow.

"What strange bosses we have nowadays," Vera muttered to herself, jangling the money in the bowl in front of her and handing out disposable paper towels. "It's really awful." She liked to pretend she took everything that happened in just the same way as some abstract Vera working as a cleaner in a toilet ought to take it, and she tried to forget that she herself had stirred up these forces of the underworld, stirred them up for no more than a joke, just so that she could have a picture hanging on the wall (as far as the music was concerned, she felt that wish had already been granted in the two accordions it included). Where Vera's life had previously been boring and monotonous, it was now eventful and full of meaning. Quite often now Vera saw various remarkable people, such as scientists, cosmonauts, and performers, and once the toilet was even visited by the father of a fraternal nation, General Pot Mir Soup, who was caught short on his way to the Kremlin. He had masses of people with him, and while he was sitting in the stall, three touchingly made-up Young Pioneers played a mournful, drawn-out melody on long flutes right beside Vera's booth. It was so moving that Vera shed a furtive tear.

One day soon after this incident Vera's boss arrived with a cassette deck and speakers, and the following day the toilet had music. Vera now had the additional responsibility of turning the cassettes over and changing them. The morning usually began with Giuseppe Verdi's "Requiem," and the first excited visitors usually appeared when the passionate soprano in the second movement was imploring the Lord to save her from eternal death.

"*Libera me domini de morte aeterna*," Vera sang along quietly, jangling the copper in her bowl in time with the powerful blows of the invisible orchestra. After that they usually put on Bach's "Christmas Oratorio" or something of the kind, something spiritual in German, and Vera, who could only follow that language with a certain effort, listened as the thin-voiced children merrily gave the Lord who had dispatched them to the world below an assurance of something or other.

"Then for what has the Lord created us?" inquired the doubting soprano, forcefully escorted by two violins.

"In order," the choir replied confidently, "that we might glorify him."

"Can this be so?" the soprano queried with renewed doubt.

"Beyond all doubting!" the children's voices sang in confirmation.

Then, as the time approached two or three o'clock, Vera would put on Mozart, and her troubled soul would slowly settle into calmness as it glided over the cold marble floor of an immense hall, in which two grand pianos jangled against each other in a minor key. When the evening was really close, Vera put on Wagner, and for a few seconds the Valkyries were confused in their flight into battle by the sight of tiled walls and sinks flickering past beneath their wildly careering steeds.

Everything would have been just wonderful, if not for one strange thing, which at first was hardly noticeable, in fact it almost seemed like a hallucination. Vera began to notice a strange smell, or to put it more bluntly, a stink, to which she had not paid any attention before. For some inexplicable reason the stink appeared when the music began to play, or rather, that was when it manifested itself. It was there all the rest of the time as well, in fact it was a fundamental element of the place, but it went pretty well unnoticed as long as it remained in harmony with everything else. When the pictures appeared on the walls, though, and then on top of that they started playing music, she began to smell that genuine, inexpressible toilet stench that no words can possibly describe, and which is merely hinted at even by the phrase "Mayakovsky's Paris."

One evening Manyasha dropped in to see Vera and while they listened to the overture to *The Corsair*, she suddenly noticed the stink as well.

"Vera," she asked, "have you never thought about how our will and imagination form these lavatories around us?"

"I have thought about it," Vera answered. "I've been thinking about it for ages and I can't understand it. I know what you're going to say. You're going to say that we ourselves create the world around us and the reason we're sitting in a public lavatory lies in our own souls. Then you'll say there really isn't any public lavatory, there isn't anything but a projection of inner content on to external object, and what seems like a stink is simply an exteriorized component of the soul. Then you'll quote something from Sologub . . ."

"And heaven's lamps to me proclaimed," Manyasha interrupted her in a sing-song voice, "that I created nature . . ."

"That's it, or something like it. Am I right?"

"Not entirely. You're making your usual mistake. The fact is that the only interesting thing about solipsism is its practical side. You've already managed to do something in this line—this picture with the troika, for example, or these dulcimers—zing, zing! But that stink, why, at what precise moment, do we create that?"

"From the practical point of view I can tell you for certain that it's no problem for me to clean up the stink, and the toilet as well."

"Me too," Manyasha answered, "I clean up the toilet every

evening. But what would come after that? Do you really think it's possible?"

Vera was about to open her mouth to reply, but she suddenly began coughing into her palm, and then carried on coughing for a long time. Manyasha stuck her tongue out at her.

Two or three days went by, and then the green curtains at the entrance were thrust aside by a group of visitors who immediately reminded Vera of that first group, in denim jackets, that had started everything happening. These people were dressed in leather and were even more ruddy-faced, but apart from that they behaved exactly the same as the first group. Soon Vera learned that they were closing down the toilet and turning the place into a shop selling goods on commission.

They kept her on as cleaner this time too, and even gave her paid leave while the repairs were going on, so that Vera got a good rest and reread several books on solipsism that she hadn't been able to get around to for ages. When she went back to work the first day, there was nothing left to remind her that the place had once been a toilet. Now just to the right of the entrance there was a long row of shelves where they sold all sorts of knick-knacks. Further in, where the urinals used to be, was a long counter, with a display stand and electronics counter opposite it. Hanging at the far end of the hall were winter clothes—leather raincoats and jackets, sheepskin coats and ladies' coats, and behind each counter stood a salesgirl. There was a lot less work for her to do now, and just loads of money. Vera now walked around the premises in a new blue overall coat, politely pushing her way through the crowd of customers and wiping the glass surfaces of the counters with a dry flannel rag. Glimmering and glittering behind the glass, like bright, multicolored Christmas-tree tinsel ("All the thoughts of the centuries! All the dreams! All the worlds!" Vera whispered to herself) lay various brands of chewing gum and condoms, plastic clip-on earrings and brooches, spectacles, hand mirrors, jewelry chains and elegant little pencils. After that, during the lunch break, she had to sweep up the dirt that the customers brought in, and then she could take it easy until evening.

Now the music played the whole day long—sometimes even several different types of music—and the stink had disappeared, as Vera proudly informed Manyasha one day when she appeared through the door in the wall. Manyasha frowned.

"I'm afraid it's not quite that simple. Of course, from one point of view, we really do create our own surroundings, but from another, we ourselves are merely the reflection of all that surrounds us. And therefore the fate of any individual in any country repeats in metaphorical terms what happens to that country—while what happens to the country is made up of thousands of separate lives."

"So what?" Vera asked, puzzled. "What's that got to do with what we're talking about?"

"Well, this," said Manyasha. "You tell me that the stink has disappeared. But it hasn't really disappeared at all. You're going to come up against it again."

Since they had transferred the men's toilet to Manyasha's side and combined it with the women's, Manyasha had changed a great deal—she spoke less and she came visiting less often too. She herself explained this by the fact that she had achieved equilibrium between Yin and Yang, but in her heart of hearts Vera believed her heavy work load and her envy of Vera's new lifestyle were really to blame—an envy that was merely masked by her philosophical attitude.

Through all of this, Vera gave not a single thought to the person who had taught her everything required to achieve this metamorphosis. Manyasha sensed Vera's changed attitude toward her, but she took it calmly, as though that was the way things ought to be—and she simply came to visit less often. Vera soon came to realize that Manyasha was right, and it happened like this: one day as she was straightening up after wiping down the glass counter, she noticed something strange out of the corner of her eye—a man smeared all over with shit. He was carrying himself with great dignity as the crowd parted before him on his way to the electronics counter. Vera shuddered and even dropped her feather duster, but when she turned her head for a better look at the man, it turned out to be nothing but a trick of the light—he was actually wearing a russet-brown leather jacket.

After that first instance, however, tricks of the light began to happen more and more often. Vera would see crumpled pieces of paper on the glass surface of the counter, and she would have to stare hard for a few seconds before she could see them as anything else. She began to feel it was no accident that the expensive decorative bottles with the fairy tale names—each of them costing three or four Soviet monthly salaries—stood on the long shelf behind the salesgirl in exactly the same spot where the urinals used to gurgle so boisterously. Even the very name "toiletries" scrawled on cardboard with a red felt tip pen suddenly became a mere euphemism. Behind the walls now there was something rumbling quietly but menacingly almost all the time, like a whispering giant; although the sound was not loud, it conveyed a sense of incredible power.

Vera began looking carefully at customers as they came in. The first thing she noticed were certain oddities in their dress: certain things they wore simply insisted on resembling shit, or just the opposite, the shit daubed on them simply insisted on resembling certain things. Many of their faces were smeared with shit in the form of dark glasses; it covered their shoulders in the form of leather jackets and encased their legs in the form of jeans. They were all smeared with it to a greater or lesser degree: three or four of them were completely covered from head to toe, and one had several layers; the crowd showed him very particular respect.

There were lots of children running around. One boy reminded Vera very much of her brother, who drowned at a Young Pioneer Camp, and she watched very carefully to see what would happen to him. At first he simply used to tell the customers what they could buy from each of the shit-smeared individuals, and he would even run up to customers as they came in and ask them:

"What do you want?"

Soon he was selling trinkets himself, and then one day, as Vera was shifting her bucket across the floor toward the counter with the huge black lumps of shit with serious-sounding Japanese names, she looked up and saw his face beaming with happiness. Looking down, she saw that his feet, which had been wearing shoes, were now thickly plastered with the same substance that covered most of the people standing around him. In a purely instinctive response she ran her duster over the boy, and the next moment he shoved her away rudely.

"Watch where you're going, you old fool," he said, brandishing the finger he had taken out of his pocket, and then, after a second's thought, transforming the gesture into a fist. Vera suddenly realized that while she was ruling the universe, old age had overtaken her, and now all that lay ahead was death.

Vera had not seen Manyasha for a long time. Recently their relationship had become a lot cooler, and the door in the wall that led to Manyasha's half of the premises remained locked for long periods. Vera began trying to recall the circumstances under which Manyasha usually appeared, and discovered that she could say nothing on that score except that sometimes she simply did.

Vera began recounting the history of their acquaintance to herself, and the longer she spent remembering, the more convinced she became that Manyasha was to blame for everything. Just exactly what this "everything" was she would hardly have been able to say, but she decided to take her revenge anyway, and began preparing a treat for the next meeting with Manyasha— that was how she thought of this thing she was preparing, a "treat," not even calling things by their real names to herself, as though behind the wall Manyasha might be frightened by reading her thoughts and decide not to come.

Manyasha evidently didn't read anything from behind the wall, because one evening she turned up. She seemed tired and unsociable, which Vera automatically explained by the fact that she had so much work to do. Forgetting about her plans for the moment, Vera told Manyasha about her hallucinations, and Manyasha livened up a bit.

"That's natural enough," she said. "After all, you understand the mystery of life, which means you can perceive the metaphysical function of objects. But since you don't know the meaning of life, you can't distinguish their metaphysical essence. And so you think that what you see is a hallucination. Have you tried explaining it for yourself?"

"No," said Vera, after a moment's thought. "It's very difficult to understand. Probably there's something that turns things into shit. It affects some things and it doesn't affect others—no— A-ha—I think I've got it now. The things themselves are not actually shit. It's when they find their way in here that they—or not even that—the shit that we live in becomes visible when it gets onto them. . . ."

"That's a bit nearer the mark," said Manyasha.

"Oh, my God—There was I thinking about pictures and music, and all the time this place was just a toilet; what music could there possibly be in here. But whose fault is it? As far as the shit's concerned, it's clear enough, it was the Communists who opened the valve."

"In what sense?" Manyasha asked.

"In both senses. No, if there's anyone to blame, Manyasha, then it's you," Vera concluded unexpectedly, and gave her former friend an unfriendly look, such a very unfriendly look that Manyasha took a small step backwards.

"Why me? On the contrary, how many times have I told you that all these mysteries would do you no good unless you came to grips with their meaning? Vera, what are you doing?"

Looking down and off to the side somewhere, Vera advanced on Manyasha, and Manyasha backed away, until they came to the narrow, awkward door leading to Manyasha's half of the premises. Manyasha stopped and lifted her eyes to Vera's face.

"Vera, what have you decided to do?"

"I want to smash your head in with an ax," Vera replied in a crazed voice, and from under her overall coat she pulled out her terrible treat, with a projection for extracting nails sprouting from its heel.

"Right across the braid, just like in Dostoyevsky."

"Well, of course, you can do that," Manyasha said nervously, "but I warn you, if you do, you'll never see me again."

"That much I can work out for myself, I'm not a total idiot," Vera whispered exaltedly as she swung her arm and brought down the ax with all her strength on Manyasha's gray head. There was a ringing and a rumbling, and Vera fainted.

When she came to she found herself lying in the changing room clutching the ax in her hands, with a tall mirror almost the height of a man, towering over her, and in it a gaping hole with the contours of an immense snowflake.

"Yesenin," thought Vera.

What frightened her most of all was that there was no door in the wall, and now she had no idea what to do with all those memories which involved the door. But even this ceased to be important when Vera suddenly realized that she herself had changed. It was as though part of her soul had disappeared, a part that she had only just become aware of, in the same way that some people are tormented by pain in amputated limbs. Everything still seemed to be in the right place, but the most important thing, which lent meaning to all the rest, had disappeared. Vera felt as though it had been replaced by a two-dimensional drawing on paper, and her two-dimensional soul generated a two-dimensional hatred for the two-dimensional world around her.

"Just you wait," she whispered to no one in particular, "I'll show you."

Her hatred was reflected in her surroundings: there was something shuddering behind the wall, and the customers in the

shop, or the toilet, or the subterranean niche where she had spent
her entire life—Vera was no longer sure of anything—would
sometimes break off their inspection of the shit plastered along
the shelves and look around in startled anxiety.

Some tremendous force was pressing against the walls from
the outside; there was something trembling and quivering behind
the thin surface as it flexed inwards—as though some immense
fist was squeezing a paper cup on the bottom of which Vera's tiny
figure was sitting, surrounded by counters and changing rooms,
squeezing it only gently as yet, but capable at any moment of totally crushing Vera's entire reality. One day, at precisely 19:40
(the exact moment when Vera thought the green figures on the
three identical lumps of shit on the shelf were showing the year
of her birth), this moment came.

Vera was standing holding her bucket, facing the long counter
with the clothes—where the sheepskin coats, leather rain slickers,
and obscene pink blouses hung jumbled together—looking ab-
sentmindedly at the customers as they fingered the sleeves and col-
lars that were so close and yet so far beyond their reach, when she
felt a sudden jab of piercing pain in her heart. Instantly, the rumbling outside became unbearably loud. The walls began to trem-
ble; they bulged inwards, then cracked open. And flowing out of
the crack, overturning the counter with the clothes as it advanced
on the terrified shrieking people, came a repulsive black-brown
flood tide.

"Aagh!" Vera just had time to sigh before she was lifted from
the floor, whirled around, and flung hard against the wall. The
last memory retained by her consciousness was the word "Karma"
written in large black letters on a white background in the same
typeface as the title of the newspaper *Pravda*. She was brought
back to her senses by another blow, this time a weak one, as she
came into contact with some twigs. The twigs proved to be on the
branches of a tall old oak tree, and for a moment Vera was at a
loss to understand how, from her position on a tiled floor she
knew every inch of, she could have been thrown up against any

branches. It turned out that she was floating along Tverskoy Boulevard on a foul-smelling, black-brown flood which was already lapping at the windows on the second and third stories of the buildings. Glancing around, she caught sight of something that looked like a hill rising up above the surface of the slurry, formed by a fountain that sprang from the very spot where her underground passage had been.

The current carried Vera on in the direction of Tverskaya Street. The surface of the slurry was rising at a fantastic speed, the two- and three-story houses at the side of the road were no longer visible, and the huge ugly theater next to them resembled an island of gray granite. Standing on the brink of its towering shoreline were three women in white muslin dresses and an officer of the White Guards who was shading his eyes as he gazed into the distance. Vera realized they must have been performing *The Three Sisters*.

She was borne on further and further. A stroller drifted past her, carrying a baby dressed in a blue cap with a big red star, who stared around in wide-eyed astonishment. Then she found herself at the corner of a house crowned by a round columned turret, on which two fat soldiers in peaked caps with blue bands were hastily readying a machine gun for firing. Finally the current carried her out onto Tverskaya Street, which was almost totally submerged, and off in the direction of the somber distant peaks with their summits crowned by barely visible ruby-red pentagrams.

The flood tide was flowing faster now. Behind her to the right, above the roofs protruding from the brownish black lava, she could see an immense rumbling geyser that obscured half the sky; its rumbling mingled with the barely distinguishable chatter of a machine gun.

"Blessed is he who has visited this world," Vera whispered, "in its fateful moments. . . ."

She saw a globe of the earth floating alongside her, and realized that it must have come from the wall of the Central Tele-

graph Building. She rowed it over to her and grabbed hold of
Scandinavia. The electric motor that turned the globe had obviously also been ripped from the wall of the Central Telegraph,
and it lent the entire structure stability—on her second attempt
Vera managed to scramble up onto its blue dome, seat herself on
the red highlighted surface of the workers' state, and look around
her.

Away in the distance she could see the television tower at Ostankino, some roofs still visible as islands, and ahead a red star
seemed to be drifting toward her over the surface of the water;
when Vera drew level with it, its lower points were already below
the surface. She grabbed hold of one of its cold glass ribs and
brought her globe to a standstill. Alongside her on the surface of
the slurry there were two soldier's caps and a soaked tie, blue with
small white polka dots—they weren't moving, which suggested
that the current here was weak.

Vera took another look around and was amazed for a moment
at the ease with which a centuries-old city had disappeared, until
the thought came to her that all changes in history, when they
happen, take place exactly like that: as though they are entirely
natural. She didn't want to think at all; she wanted to sleep, and
stretched out on the convex surface of the USSR, resting her
head on her mop-callused hand.

When she woke, the world consisted of two parts—the early
evening sky and an infinite smooth surface, which had turned
quite black in the dim light. There was nothing else to be seen,
the ruby-red stars had long ago sunk out of sight and God only
knew what depth they were at now. Vera thought of Atlantis, then
about the Moon and its ninety-six laws, but all of these comfortable, familiar old thoughts, inside which only yesterday her soul
could nestle and curl up into a tight ball, were out of place now,
and Vera dozed off again. Through her drowsiness she suddenly
noticed how quiet it was—she noticed because she heard a gentle
splashing coming from the direction where the magnificent red
hill of the sunset rose up above the horizon.

An inflatable dinghy was moving towards her, with a tall, broad-shouldered figure in a peaked cap standing in it, holding a long oar. Vera pushed herself up with her hands, thinking as she looked at the approaching figure that on her globe she must look like an allegorical figure; she even realized what the allegory was—it was an allegory of herself, drifting on a globe with a dubious history across the boundless ocean of existence. Or of nonexistence—but that made no difference at all. The boat drew close, and Vera recognized the man standing in it. It was Marshal Pot Mir Soup.

"Vera," he said, with a strong Eastern accent, "do you know who I am?"

There was something unnatural about his voice.

"I know," answered Vera, "I've read a bit. I realized everything a long time ago, only there was a tunnel through what I read. There has to be to be some kind of tunnel."

"That can be arranged."

Vera felt the surface of the globe she was riding open inward, and she tumbled into the gap. It happened very quickly. She managed to get a grip on the edge of the breach, and began flailing her feet to find some support, but there was nothing beneath her but black emptiness into which the wind blew. Above her head there remained a patch of the mournful evening sky, shaped exactly like the outline of the USSR (her fingers were straining with all their might against the southern border). The familiar silhouette—which all her life had reminded her of a beef carcass hanging on the wall of the meat department in her local food store—suddenly seemed the most beautiful thing it was possible to imagine. And apart from it there was nothing else left at all.

From out of the fleeting world, Vera heard a splash, and a heavy oar struck her right, and then her left hand. The bright silhouette of the motherland swirled away and disappeared into the distance far below. Vera felt herself floating in a strange space—it couldn't really be called falling because there was no air, and even more importantly, because she herself was not actually there. She tried to catch a glimpse of at least some part of her body and failed, although she was staring at her arms and legs.

There was nothing left but this looking, and it didn't see anything even though the looking, as Vera realized with a fright, was in all directions at once, and there was no need at all to try and look in any particular direction. Then Vera noticed that she could hear voices—but not with her ears, she was simply aware of someone else's distant conversation. It concerned herself.

"There's one here with third degree solipsism," said what seemed to be a low and rumbling voice. "What do we recommend for that?"

"Solipsism?" broke in what might have been another voice, thin and high pitched. "That's not very pleasant at all. Eternal confinement in the prose of socialist realism. As a character."

"There's no vacancies left," said the low voice.

"What about Sholokhov's Cossacks?" the high voice asked hopefully.

"Full up."

"Then what about that, what do they call it . . ." the high voice began enthusiastically, "war prose? Maybe some two-paragraph Lieutenant in the NKVD? Does nothing but appear around the corner, wiping the sweat from her brow, and gazing piercingly at the bystanders? Nothing there at all except a cap, sweat, and a piercing gaze? For the rest of eternity, eh?"

"I told you, there's no room left."

"Then what is to be done?"

"Let her tell us," the low voice rumbled in the very center of Vera's being. "Hey, Vera! What is to be done?"

"What is to be done?" Vera repeated. "What do you mean what is to be done?"

Suddenly it felt as though a wind had risen—it wasn't real wind, but it reminded Vera of it, because she felt herself being carried off somewhere like a floating leaf.

"What is to be done?" Vera repeated out of sheer inertia, and then suddenly understood what was happening.

"Mmm!" the low voice growled tenderly.

"What is to be done?" Vera screamed in horror. "What is to be done?"

Every scream lent strength to this likeness of the wind; she hurtled through emptiness with ever-increasing speed, and after the third scream she sensed that she had entered the gravitational field of some immense object which had not existed before the scream, but which became so real after it that she found herself hurtling toward it as if falling out a window.

"What is to be done?" she screamed for the last time, before crashing into something with terrifying force.

She fell asleep at the moment of impact—and through her sleep she could hear a monotonous, mechanical-sounding voice:

". . . the position of assistant manager, I set the following condition: that I can start the job when I want, in a month or two, say. I want to make good use of the time off. I haven't seen the old folks in Ryazan for five years—I'll go visit them. Goodbye, Verochka. Don't get up. There'll be time tomorrow. Sleep."

Chernyshevsky, *What Is To be Done?*, Chapter XXVII:

When Vera Pavlovna emerged from her room the following day, her husband and Masha were already packing two suitcases.

Tai Shou Chuan USSR
(A Chinese Folk Tale)

AS EVERYONE KNOWS, OUR
universe is located in the teapot of a certain Lui Dunbin who
sells trinkets at the bazaar in Chanyan. The strange thing is, however, that Chanyan ceased to exist several centuries ago. For many
ages already there has been no Lui Dunbin sitting in the bazaar,
and long, long ago his teapot was melted down or squashed as flat
as a pancake by the weight of the earth above it. In my opinion
there is only one rational explanation which may be offered for
this strange contradiction in terms—that the universe continues
to exist, while its location has already perished: while Lui Dunbin was still dozing at his stall in the bazaar, in his teapot they
were already excavating the ruins of ancient Chanyan, the grass
was growing thick above his grave and people were launching
rockets into space, winning and losing wars, building telescopes
and tank factories . . . Stop . . . This is where we shall start.
In his childhood, Ch'an the Seventh was called the Little Red
Star. Then he grew up and went to work in the commune.

What is the life of a peasant? This is something we all know.
Like others, Ch'an lost heart and took to drinking without re-
straint. He even lost track of time. He got drunk in the morning
and hid in the empty rice barn in the yard of his own house, so
that the chairman Fu Yuishi, nicknamed "the Bronze Engels" for

his great political understanding and physical strength, would not notice him. Ch'an hid because the Bronze Engels often accused drunks of certain incomprehensible offenses—of conformism or degeneracy—and forced them to work without pay. People were afraid to argue with him because he called that a declaration of counterrevolutionary views and sabotage, and counterrevolutionary saboteurs were supposed to be sent to the city.

That morning, as usual, Ch'an and the others were lying around drunk in their barns and the Bronze Engels was riding around the empty streets on a donkey, looking for someone he could send to work. Ch'an was in a really bad way, and he lay with his belly to the ground and his head covered with an empty rice sack. There were several ants crawling across his face, and one even crawled into his ear, but Ch'an was in no state to raise his hand to crush them, his hangover was too bad. Suddenly from far away, from the Party yamen itself, where there was a loudspeaker, he heard the time signal on the radio. Seven times the gong sounded, and then. . . .

Either Ch'an imagined it, or a long black limousine actually did draw up at the barn. It was a mystery how it could ever have gotten in through the gate. Out of it emerged two fat bureaucrats in dark clothing with square ears and little badges in the form of red flags, while a third person with a gold star on his chest and a prawnlike mustache, remained sitting in the depths of the car, fanning himself with a red file for papers. The first two waved their hands and came into the barn. Ch'an threw the sack off his head and stared at his visitors in total incomprehension. One of them came over to Ch'an, kissed him three times on the lips and said:

"We have come to you from the distant land of the USSR. Our Son of Bread has heard much of your great talents and sense of justice and he invites you to visit him."

Ch'an had never even heard of such a country. "Maybe," he thought, "the Bronze Engels has informed against me, and they're taking me in for sabotage? They say they like to play the fool when they do that . . ."

In his fear Ch'an broke into a fierce sweat.

"And who are you?" he asked.

"We are P.A.'s," the strangers replied, then they took Ch'an by his shirt and pants, threw him onto the back seat, and sat on each side of him. Ch'an made as though to leap out again, but he received such a blow to the ribs that he quickly changed his mind and submitted. The driver started the engine, and the car moved off.

It was a strange journey. At first they appeared to be driving along the familiar road, then suddenly they turned off into the forest and seemed to dive down into a pit. The car was jolted hard, and Ch'an squeezed his eyes tight shut. When he opened them again, he saw that they were driving along a broad highway flanked by small houses with aerials on their roofs. There were cows wandering about and tall posters with pictures of the fleshy faces of ancient rulers and inscriptions in an ancient tadpole script. All of this seemed to come together over their heads, and it was as though the road was passing through an immense empty pipe. "It's like inside the barrel of a cannon," Ch'an thought for some reason.

It was amazing. He'd spent all of his life in the village and never even suspected that there were places like this nearby. It was clear now that they weren't going to the city and Ch'an felt calmer. The journey proved to be a long one. After a couple of hours Ch'an began to nod off, and then he fell asleep altogether. He dreamed that the Bronze Engels had lost his Party Card and he, Ch'an, had been appointed chairman of the commune in his place and now he was walking along the deserted dusty street looking for someone he could send to work. As he came up to his own house, he thought:

"Right then, Ch'an the Seventh is probably lying drunk in the barn—I'll just glance inside and see." He seemed to remember that he was the Ch'an the Seventh himself, but he still had this thought. Ch'an was quite amazed at this, even in his dream, but he decided that if he'd been made chairman, he must first have studied the art of Party vigilance, and this was it. He walked up to the barn, opened the door and there, sure enough, he saw himself sleeping in the corner, with a sack over his head. "Just you wait," thought Ch'an, and he picked up the half-empty bottle of beer from the floor and poured the contents straight onto the back of the head under the sack.

Suddenly there was a whirring and screeching and knocking sound above his head and Ch'an waved his arms in the air and woke up. It turned out they'd switched on some gadget on the roof of the car that whirled around and blinked and howled. Now all the cars and people ahead of them began to give way, and the constables with striped batons saluted. Ch'an's two companions flushed in pleasure. Ch'an dozed off again, and when he woke it was already dark, the car was standing on a beautiful square in a strange city and there were crowds of people all around, but a line of constables in black caps prevented them from coming close.

"Perhaps you should go out to the workers?" one of Ch'an's traveling companions said with a smile. Ch'an had noticed that the further they left his village behind them, the more politely the pair of them treated him.

"Where are we?" Ch'an asked.

"This is Pushkin Square in the city of Moscow," one of the P.A.'s answered and pointed to a heavy metal figure that was clearly visible in the beams of the searchlights beside a column of water that glittered as it scattered in drops into the air.

Above the monument and the fountain words of fire blazed across the sky. Ch'an got out of the car. Several searchlights illuminated the crowd, and above their heads he could see immense banners: "GREETINGS TO COMRADE SALAMI FROM THE WORKERS OF MOSCOW!"

Also floating above the heads of the crowd were portraits of himself on long poles. Ch'an suddenly realized that he could read the tadpole script without any difficulty, and he couldn't even understand why it was called tadpole, but before he could come to terms with his surprise a small group of people squeezed through the police cordon and came towards him: there were two women in red sarafans reaching down to the asphalt with semicircles of tin on their heads and two men in military uniform with sawn-off balalaikas. Ch'an realized that these must be the workers. They were carrying something held out in front of them, something small, dark, and round, like the front wheel of a Shanghai tractor. One of the P.A.'s whispered in Ch'an's ear that this was the so-called bread and salt greeting. Following his instructions, Ch'an tossed a piece of the bread into his mouth and kissed one of the girls on her rouged cheek, scraping his forehead on the tin kokoshnik in the process.

Then the police orchestra rumbled into life, playing on strangely shaped *tsins* and *yuahs*, and the crowded square yelled as one: "Hoo-rr-aaah!"

Actually, some of them were shouting that they should beat someone called yids, but Ch'an was not acquainted with the local customs, and so he decided not to ask about that.

"Who is Comrade Salami?" he inquired, when they had left the square behind them.

"You are Comrade Salami now," the P.A. replied.

"Why am I?"

"The Son of Bread has decided," replied the P.A. "The country is short of meat, and our ruler believes that if his deputy has a name like that, the workers will be calmer."

"But what happened to his old deputy?" Ch'an asked.

"The previous deputy," the P.A. replied, "looked like a pig; they often used to show him on the television, and for a while the workers would forget that there wasn't enough meat. But then the Son of Bread learned that his deputy was concealing the fact that his head had been cut off a long time ago, and he was employing the services of a sorcerer.

"But then how could they show him on television if his head had been cut off?" asked Ch'an.

"That was precisely what offended the workers most," the P.A. said, and then fell silent.

Ch'an wanted to ask what happened after that and why the P.A. always called the people workers, but he decided not to, in case he put his foot in it somehow. Soon the car came to a stop at a large brick house.

"This is where you are going to live, Comrade Salami," said one of the P.A.'s.

Ch'an was shown into his apartment, which was decorated in an expensively luxurious style, but which gave him a bad feeling—as if the rooms were spacious and the windows were big and the furniture was beautiful, but somehow it was all unreal; there was something dark and devilish about it, as though you only had to clap your hands hard and it would all disappear. But then the P.A.'s took off their jackets, vodka and meat hors d'oeuvres appeared on the table, and a few minutes later Ch'an could have looked the devil in the eye and spat at him. The P.A.'s rolled up their sleeves, one of them picked up a guitar and began to play, and the other began to sing in a pleasant voice:

> We are children of the Cosmos
> But first of all
> We are your children, Mother Earth!

Ch'an couldn't quite grasp whose children they were, but he was beginning to like them more and more. They juggled and tumbled very skillfully, and when Ch'an clapped and applauded, they recited freedom-loving verse and sang beautiful songs about strong male friendship and the beauty of little girls. And there was a song about something incomprehensible that wrung Ch'an's heart when he listened to it.

When Ch'an woke, it was morning. One of the P.A.'s was shaking him by the shoulder. Ch'an felt ashamed when he saw what condition he had slept in, especially since the P.A.'s were neat and freshly washed.

"The First Deputy has arrived!" one of them said.

Ch'an noticed that his patched blue jacket had disappeared, and in its place on the chair hung a gray jacket with a little red flag on the lapel. He began dressing hurriedly, and had just finished tying the knot in his tie when a smallish man sporting noble gray locks was led into the room.

"Comrade Salami!" he announced, "the foundation of the wheel is the spoke; the foundation of order in the Empire is personnel; the reliability of the wheel depends on the space between the spokes, and personnel decide everything. The Son of Bread knows of you as a noble and enlightened man and he wishes to elevate you to high office."

"How could I dare to dream of such an honor?" responded Ch'an, barely managing to suppress his hiccuping.

The First Deputy invited him to follow. They went downstairs, got into a black car, and set off along the street, which was called Great Armory Street. Then they found themselves in front of a house like the one where Ch'an had spent the night, only several times larger. The house was surrounded by a large park. The First Deputy went ahead along the narrow pathway. Ch'an followed him, listening to the P.A. hurrying along behind playing a small flute in the form of a fountain pen.

The moon was shining. Black swans of amazing beauty were swimming in a pond, and Ch'an was informed that they were all actually enchanted KGB agents. There were paratroopers disguised as marines lurking behind the poplars and willows. There were marines lying in the bushes, disguised as paratroopers. At the entrance to the house several old women sitting on a bench ordered them in men's voices to halt and lie on the ground with their hands on the back of their heads. Only the First Deputy and Ch'an were admitted. They walked for a long time through corridors and up staircases on which happy smartly-dressed children played, and finally they approached a pair of tall inlaid and encrusted doors at which two cosmonauts with flamethrowers stood on guard.

Ch'an was alarmed and crushed by such magnificence. The First Deputy pushed open a ponderous door and said to Ch'an: "After you."

Ch'an heard gentle music and he tiptoed inside, where he found himself in a bright spacious room with windows wide open to the sky. In the very center, seated at a white grand piano, was the Son of Bread, covered in ears of corn and gold stars. He could see right away that this was no ordinary man. He was connected by several pipes to a large metal cabinet beside him which was gurgling quietly. The Son of Bread glanced at the new arrivals, but did not seem to see them; the wind came in at the windows and ruffled his gray hair. In fact he had seen everything, and a minute later he raised his hands from the piano, smiled graciously and spoke:

"In order to strengthen . . ."

He spoke indistinctly and seemed to be short of breath, and Ch'an realized that now he would be an extremely important official. Then came lunch. Ch'an had never eaten anything so delicious. The Son of Bread did not put so much as a single morsel in his own mouth. Instead, the P.A.'s opened a small door in the cabinet, threw in several shovels of caviar and poured in a bottle of wheat wine. Ch'an could never have imagined anything like that happening. After lunch he and the First Deputy thanked the ruler of the USSR and went out.

He was driven home, and in the evening there was a festive concert, at which Ch'an was seated in the very front row. The concert was a magnificent sight—every piece involved an amazing number of players in incredibly close coordination. Ch'an particularly liked the children's patriotic dance "My Heavy Machine Gun" and "The Song of the Triune Goal" as performed by the State Choir, except that during the performance of the song they trained a green floodlight on the soloist and his face became quite corpselike, but then Ch'an did not know all the local customs, so he did not ask his P.A.'s about anything.

In the morning, as he drove around the city, Ch'an saw

crowds of people stretching along the streets. One P.A. explained that all of these people had come to vote for Pyotr Semyonovich Salami, that is, for him, Ch'an. In a fresh newspaper Ch'an saw his own portrait with his biography, which said that he had a third-level education and had previously worked as a diplomat. That was how in year eighteen of government under the motto of "Efficiency and Quality," Ch'an the Seventh became an important official in the USSR.

A new life opened up. Ch'an had nothing at all to do, nobody asked him about anything, and nobody required anything of him. Occasionally he would be summoned to one of Moscow's palaces, where he sat in silence on the presidium as some song or dance was performed. At first he felt extremely embarrassed that so many people were watching him, but then he took a look at how the others behaved, and began acting the same as they did, hiding half of his face behind his hand, and nodding thoughtfully at the most unexpected moments.

He acquired a circle of high-living friends: People's Artists, Academicians, and General Directors skilled in the martial arts. Ch'an himself became a Victor of Socialist Competition and a Hero of Socialist Labor. In the mornings they all got drunk and went to the Bolshoi Theater to indulge in debauchery with the singers. Of course, if someone more important than Ch'an was taking his revels there, they had to turn back, and then they would stagger into some restaurant, and if the simple people or even the bureaucrats saw the sign "Special Party Service" hanging on the door, then they understood that it was Ch'an and his company making merry, and they kept well away. Ch'an also liked making trips to the botanical gardens to admire the flowers. On those occasions, Ch'an's bodyguards would ring the Gardens to make sure the ordinary people didn't get in his way.

The workers respected and feared Ch'an a great deal; they sent him thousands of letters complaining of injustice and asking him to help with all kinds of matters. Ch'an would sometimes pull some letter or other out of the heap at random and then help—this earned him a good reputation with the people.

What Ch'an liked most of all was not the free food and drink, not all his mansions and mistresses, but the local people, the workers. They were hard-working and modest, understanding. For instance, Ch'an could crush as many of them as he liked under the wheels of his immense black limousine, and everyone who happened to be on the streets at the time would turn away, knowing that it was none of their business, and the main thing was that they must not be late for work. They were so very self-less, just like ants. Ch'an even wrote an article for the main news-paper—"With People Like This You Can Do Anything You Want"—and they published it, with just a slight change to the title which became, "With People Like This You Can Achieve Great Things." That was more or less what Ch'an had wanted to say. The Son of Bread was extremely fond of Ch'an. He would often summon him and burble something to him, but Ch'an couldn't understand a single word. In the cabinet something gur-gled and glubbed, and the Son of Bread looked worse with every day that passed. Ch'an felt extremely sorry for him, but there was nothing he could do to help.

One day, as Ch'an was resting on his estate outside Moscow, news arrived of the death of the Son of Bread. Ch'an took fright and thought that now he was bound to be seized and arrested. He wanted to strangle himself on the spot, but his servants per-suaded him to wait for a while, and in fact nothing terrible hap-pened at all. On the contrary, he was appointed to yet another post: now he was in charge of the country's entire fishing indus-try. Several friends of Ch'an's were arrested, and a new leader-ship was established under the motto "Renewal of the Origins." During these days Ch'an's nerves were under such great strain that he totally forgot his own origin, and even began to believe that he really had worked as a diplomat and not spent days and nights at a stretch drinking in a small remote village. During the eighth year of rule under the motto "The Workers' Letters," Ch'an became the ruler of Moscow, and in the third year of rule under the motto "The Radiance of Truth," he married, taking as his wife the beautiful daughter of a fabulously rich academician. She was as elegant as a doll, had read many books, and knew dancing and music. Soon she bore him two sons.

The years passed and ruler followed ruler, but Ch'an only grew stronger and stronger. Gradually a large circle of devoted officials and military officers consolidated itself around him, and they began saying in low voices that it was time for Ch'an to take power into his own hands. Then one morning it happened. Ch'an now discovered the secret of the white grand piano. The Son of Bread's main responsibility was to sit at it and play some simple melody. It was considered that in doing this he set the fundamental harmony which was followed in every other part of the government of the country. Ch'an realized that the difference between rulers lay in which tunes they knew. The only thing he could remember very well was *The Dog's Waltz*, and for most of the time that was what he played. On one occasion he attempted to play the *Moonlight Sonata*, but he made several mistakes, and the following day a rebellion broke out among the tribes of the Far North, and there was an earthquake in the South, in which however, God be praised, nobody was killed. The rebellion caused quite a lot of bother, though: for five days the rebels with their black banners bearing a yellow circle fought with the "Brothers Karamazov" crack paratroop division, until they had all been killed to the last man.

After that Ch'an took no more risks and he played nothing but *The Dog's Waltz*, but he could play it any way at all—with his eyes closed, with his back to the piano, or even lying on it belly-down. In a secret drawer under the grand piano he discovered a collection of melodies composed by the rulers of ancient times, and he often leafed through it in the evenings. He learned, for instance, that on the very day the ruler Khrushchev played *The Flight of the Bumblebee*, an enemy plane was shot down over the country's territory. The notes in many of the melodies had been masked with black paint, and there was no way of telling what the rulers of those years had played. Ch'an had now become the most powerful man in the country. As the motto for his reign he chose the words "The Great Reconciliation." Ch'an's wife built new palaces, his sons grew, the people prospered, but Ch'an himself was often sad. Although there was no pleasure that he did not experience, many cares still gnawed at his heart. He begun turning gray and hearing less and less well in his left ear.

In the evenings Ch'an dressed himself up as an intellectual and wandered about the town, listening to what the people were saying. During his strolls he began to notice that no matter where he wandered, he always came out onto the same streets. They had strange names, such as Little Armory Street or Great Armory Street, they were all downtown, and the most distant street on which Ch'an ever found himself in his wanderings was called Ballbearing Street. Beyond that, they said, there was Machine Gun Street, and even further out, the First and Second Caterpillar Track Passages. But Ch'an had never been there. When he dressed up to go out he either drank in the restaurants around Pushkin Square or dropped in to see his lover on Radio Street and take her to the secret food stores on Corpse Street. (That was its real name, but in order not to frighten the workers, all of the signs there had the "r" missing.) His lover, a young ballerina, was as happy as a little girl when he did this, and Ch'an's heart felt a little lighter, and a minute later they would be back on Great Armory Street.

For some time now the strange narrowness of the world in which he moved had been grating on Ch'an's nerves. Of course there were other streets and even, it seemed, other cities and provinces, but Ch'an, as an old member of the upper ruling echelons, knew perfectly well that they existed for the most part in the empty spaces between the streets onto which he constantly emerged during his walks, simply as a blind. And although Ch'an had ruled the country for eleven years, he was an honest man, and he felt very strange making speeches about meadows and wide open spaces, when he remembered that even most of the streets in Moscow might as well not exist.

One day, however, he gathered the leadership together and said:

"Comrades! We all know that here in Moscow there are only a few real streets, and the rest hardly exist at all. And there's no knowing what lies further out, beyond the ring road. Then why . . . ?"

He had not even finished speaking before everyone there began shouting, leapt to their feet, and immediately voted to remove Ch'an from all of his posts. As soon as they had done that, the new Son of Bread climbed up on the table and shouted:

"Right, gag him and. . ."

"At least let me say good-bye to my wife and children!" Ch'an implored. But no one heard what he said. They bound him hand and foot, gagged him, and threw him into a car. After that things went as usual—they drove him to the Chinese Passage, stopped right there in the middle of the road, opened a manhole in the asphalt, and threw him in headfirst. The back of Ch'an's head struck against something and he lost consciousness.

When he opened his eyes, he saw that he was lying on the floor of his barn. He heard a gong strike twice outside and a woman's voice say:

"Beijing time, nine o'clock."

Ch'an rubbed his forehead, leapt to his feet, and staggered out onto the street, and at this very moment the Bronze Engels rode out from behind the corner. Like a fool, Ch'an panicked and ran, and the Bronze Engels rode after him with a loud clatter of hooves, past the silent houses with the lowered blinds and the locked gates. He overtook Ch'an on the village square, accused him of Ch'ungophobia, and banished him to sort magic mushrooms.

When he came back three years later, the first thing Ch'an did was to take a look around his barn. The wall on one side ran into a fence behind which there was a huge pile of garbage that had been accumulating there for as long as Ch'an could remember. There were large red ants crawling over it. Ch'an took a spade and began digging. He stuck the spade into the heap several times, and eventually it struck iron. It turned out that buried under the garbage was a Japanese tank that had been there since the war. It was standing so that the barn and the fence concealed it from view, and Ch'an could dig it out without worrying about anybody seeing it— especially as everybody was lying around drunk at home.

When Ch'an opened the hatch, his face was struck by a wave of sourness. There was a big anthill inside, and the remains of one of the tank's crew were still in the turret. When he took a closer look, Ch'an began recognizing the shapes of things. Beside the breech of the gun there was a small bronze figure dangling on a green-tarnished chain. Beside it, under the observation slit, there was a puddle where rain water collected. Ch'an recognized Pushkin Square with its monument and fountain; an empty, crumpled American can of Spam was the McDonald's restaurant, and a Coca Cola bottle cap was the same billboard Ch'an had stared at for so long with his fists clenched tight from the window of his limousine. It had all been dumped just recently by American spies on their way through the village.

For some reason the dead driver was not wearing a helmet but a forage cap that had slipped down over his ear—its cockade looked very much like the dome on the World Peace cinema. The remnants of the driver's cheeks bore long sideburns, through which numerous ants were crawling, carrying grubs. When he looked closer, Ch'an could see the two boulevards that came together at Corpse Square. He recognized many streets: Great Armory Street was the front section of armor, and Little Armory Street was the side section. There was a rusting antenna protruding from the tank, and Ch'an realized this was the Ostankino television transmitter. Ostankino itself was the corpse of the gunner and radio operator. The driver had obviously managed to escape.

Ch'an took a long stick and rummaged in the anthill to find the dam, the spot in Moscow where Mantulinskaya Street was located and nobody was ever allowed to enter. He sought out Zhukovka, where the most important dachas were—this was a big burrow, where the fat ants each three *tsuns* long wriggled along. And the ring road was the ring on which the turret turned.

Ch'an thought for minute and recalled how he had been bound and thrown head first into a sewer shaft, and he felt a mixture of fury and resentment. He made up a solution of chlorine in two buckets and poured it into the hatch. Then he closed the hatch and threw earth and rubbish over the tank the way it had been before. And soon he had forgotten all about the entire story. What is the life of a peasant? This is something that we all know. In order to avoid being accused of bearing arms in support of Japanese militarism, Ch'an never told anyone that he had a Japanese tank beside his house. He told me this story many years later when we met by chance in a train. It seemed to me to have the ring of truth, and I decided to write it down.

May all of this serve as a lesson to those who would aspire to power. If our entire Universe is located in the teapot of Lui Dunbin, then what can be said of the country which Ch'an visited? He spent no more than a moment there, and yet it seemed as though his entire life had passed. He rose all the way from prisoner to ruler, and it turned out that he had merely crawled from one burrow into another. Miracles, no more and no less. How apt are the words spoken by comrade Li Chiao of the Huachous regional committee: "A noble name, wealth, high rank, and power capable of crushing a state are, in the eyes of a wise man, little different from an anthill." In my opinion this is just as true as the fact that in the north China extends to the shore of the Arctic Ocean and in the west to the boundaries of Franco-Britain.

So Lu-Tan

THE NEW DIRECTIONS *Bibelots*

JORGE LUIS BORGES
EVERYTHING AND NOTHING

KAY BOYLE
THE CRAZY HUNTER

H.D.
KORA AND KA

SHUSAKU ENDO
FIVE BY ENDO

RONALD FIRBANK
CAPRICE

F. SCOTT FITZGERALD
THE JAZZ AGE

GUSTAVE FLAUBERT
A SIMPLE HEART

JOHN OF PATMOS
THE APOCALYPSE

FEDERICO GARCÍA LORCA
IN SEARCH OF DUENDE

THOMAS MERTON
THOUGHTS ON THE EAST

HENRY MILLER
A DEVIL IN PARADISE

YUKIO MISHIMA
PATRIOTISM

OCTAVIO PAZ
A TALE OF TWO GARDENS

VICTOR PELEVIN
4 BY PELEVIN

EZRA POUND
DIPTYCH ROME-LONDON

WILLIAM SAROYAN
FRESNO STORIES

MURIEL SPARK
THE ABBESS OF CREWE
THE DRIVER'S SEAT

DYLAN THOMAS
EIGHT STORIES

TENNESSEE WILLIAMS
THE ROMAN SPRING OF MRS. STONE

WILLIAM CARLOS WILLIAMS
ASPHODEL, THAT GREENY FLOWER &
OTHER LOVE POEMS